THE LAST CHANCE KID

Nelson Nye

GUNSMOKE

THE LAST CHANCE KID

One

MY NAME IS Alfred Addlington. Some may find it hard to believe I was born in New York City. I never knew my mother. Father is a lord; I suppose you would call him a belted earl. The family never cared for Mother. Marrying a commoner if you are of the nobility is far worse, it was felt, than murdering someone.

I was, of course, educated in England. As a child I'd been an avid reader, and always at the back of my mind was this horrible obsession to one day become a Wild West cowboy. I'd no need to run away—transportation was happily furnished. While I was in my seventeenth year my youthful peccadillos were such that I was put on a boat bound for America, made an allowance and told never to come back.

They've been hammering outside. I have been in this place now more than four months and would never have believed it could happen to me, but the bars on my window are truly there, and beyond the window they are building a gallows. So I'd better make haste if I'm to get this all down.

I do not lay my being here to a "broken home" or evil companions. I like to feel in some part it is only a matter of justice miscarried, though I suppose most any rogue faced with the rope is bound to consider himself badly

1

used. But you shall judge for yourself.

Seventeen I was when put aboard that boat, and I had a wealth of experience before at nineteen this bad thing caught up with me.

So here I was again in America. In a number of ways it was a peculiar homecoming. First thing I did after clearing customs was get aboard a train that would take me into those great open spaces I'd so long been entranced with. It brought me to New Mexico and a town called Albuquerque, really an overgrown village from which I could see the Watermellon Mountains.

I found the land and the sky and the brilliant sunshine remarkably stimulating. Unlike in the British Midlands the air was clean and crisply invigorating. But no one would have me. At the third ranch I tried they said, "Too young. We got no time to break in a raw kid with roundup scarce two weeks away."

At that time I'd no idea of the many intricacies or the harsh realities of the cow business. You might say I had on a pair of rose-colored glasses. I gathered there might be quite a ruckus building up in Lincoln County, a sort of large-scale feud from all I could learn, so I bought myself a horse, a pistol and a J. B. Stetson hat and headed for the action.

In the interests of saving time and space I'll only touch on the highlights of these preliminaries, recording full details where events became of impelling importance.

Passing through Seven Oaks, I met Billy, a chap whose name was on everyone's tongue, though I could not think him worth half the talk. To me he seemed hard, mean-spirited and stupid besides. He made fun of my horse, calling it a crowbait, declared no real gent would be found dead even near it. Turned out he knew of a first-class mount he'd be glad to secure for me if

I'd put one hundred dollars into his grubby hand. He was a swaggering sort I was glad to be rid of. Feeling that when in Rome one did as the Romans, I gave him the hundred dollars, not expecting ever to see him again, but hoping in these strange surroundings I would not be taken for a gullible "greenhorn."

A few days later another chap, who said his name was Jesse Evans, advised me to steer clear of Billy. "A bad lot," he told me. "A conniving double-crosser." When I mentioned giving Billy the hundred dollars on the understanding he would provide a top horse, he said with a snort and a kind of pitying look, "You better bid that money good-bye right now."

But three days later, true to his word, Billy rode up to the place I was lodging with a fine horse in tow. During my schooling back in England I had learned quite a bit about horses, mostly hunters and hacks and jumpers and a few that ran in "flat" races for purses, and this mount Billy fetched looked as good as the best. "Here, get on him," Billy urged. "See what you think, and if he won't do I'll find you another."

"He'll do just fine," I said, taking the lead shank, "and here's ten dollars for your kindness."

With that lopsided grin he took the ten and rode off.

I rode the new horse over to the livery and dressed him in my saddle and bridle while the proprietor eyed me with open mouth. "Don't tell me that's yours," he finally managed, still looking as if he couldn't believe what he saw.

"He surely is. Yes, indeed. Gave a hundred dollars for him."

Just as I was about to mount up, a mustached man came bustling into the place. "Stop right there!" this one said across the glint of a pistol. "I want to know what you're doing with the Major's horse. Speak up or it'll be the worse for you."

"What Major?"

"Major Murphy. A big man around here."

"Never heard of him. I bought this horse for one hundred dollars."

"Bought it, eh? Got a bill of sale?"

"Well, no," I said. "Didn't think to ask for one."

I'd discovered by this time the man with the gun had a star on his vest. His expression was on the skeptical side. He wheeled on the liveryman. "You sell him that horse?"

"Not me! Came walkin' in here with it not ten minutes ago."

"I'm goin' to have to hold you, young feller," the man with the star said, pistol still aimed at my belt buckle. "A horse thief's the lowest scoundrel I know of."

A shadow darkened the doorway just then and Jesse Evans stepped in. "Hang on a bit, Marshal. I'll vouch for this button. If he told you he paid for this horse it's the truth. Paid it to Billy—I'll take my oath on it."

A rather curious change reshaped the marshal's features. "You sure of that, Evans?"

"Wouldn't say so if I wasn't."

The marshal looked considerably put out. "All right," he said to me, "looks like you're cleared. But I'm confiscatin' this yere horse; I'll see it gits back to the rightful owner. You're free to go, but don't let me find you round here come sundown." And he went off with the horse.

"Never mind," Evans said. "Just charge it up to experience. But was I you I'd take the marshal's advice and hunt me another habitation." And he grinned at me sadly. "I mean pronto—right now."

Still rummaging my face, he said, scrubbing a fist across his own, "Tell you what I'll do," and led me away out of the livery-keeper's hearing. "I've got a reasonably good horse I'll let you have for fifty bucks. Even throw in a saddle—not so handsome as the one you had but durable and sturdy. You interested?"

Once stung, twice shy. "Let's see him," I said, and followed him out to a corral at the far edge of town. I looked the horse over for hidden defects but could find nothing wrong with it; certainly the animal should be worth fifty dollars. Firmly I said, "I'll be wanting a bill of sale."

"Of course," he chuckled. "Naturally." Fetching a little blue notebook out of a pocket, he asked politely, "What name do you go by?"

"My own," I said. "Alfred Addlington."

He wrote it down with a flourish. "All right, Alfie." He tore the page from his book and I put it in my wallet while Jesse saddled and bridled my new possession. I handed him the money, accepted the reins and stepped into the saddle.

He said, "I'll give you a piece of advice you can take or cock a snook at. Notice you're packin' a pistol. Never put a hand anyplace near it without you're aimin' to use it. Better still," he said, looking me over more sharply, "get yourself a shotgun, one with two barrels. Nobody'll laugh at that kind of authority."

"Well, thanks. Where do I purchase one?"

"Be a-plenty at Lincoln if that's where you're headed. Any gun shop'll have 'em."

I thanked him again and, having gotten precise directions, struck out for the county seat feeling I'd been lucky to run across such a good Samaritan. I was a pretty fair shot with handgun or rifle but had discovered after much practice I could be killed and buried before getting my pistol into speaking position. So Evans's advice about acquiring a shotgun seemed additional evidence of the goodwill he bore me.

It was shortly after noon the next day when I came up the dirt road into Lincoln. For all practical purposes it was a one-street town, perhaps half a mile long, flanked by business establishments, chief amongst them being the two-storey Murphy-Dolan store building. I recall wondering if this was the Major whose stolen horse Billy'd sold me, later discovering it was indeed. Leaving my horse at a hitch rack I went inside to make inquiries about finding a job.

The gentleman I talked with had an Irish face underneath a gray derby. After listening politely he informed me he was Jimmie Dolan—the Dolan of the establishment—and could offer me work as a sort of handyman if such wasn't beneath my dignity. If I showed aptitude, he said, there'd be a better job later and he would start me off at fifty cents a day.

I told him I'd take it.

"If you've a horse there's a carriage shed back of the store where you can leave him and we'll sell you oats at a discount," he added.

"I'd been hoping to get on with some ranch," I said.

"A fool's job," said Dolan with a grimace. "Long hours, hard work, poor pay and no future," he assured me. "You string your bets with us and you'll get to be somebody while them yahoos on ranches are still punchin' cows."

I went out to feed, water and put up my new horse. There was a man outside giving it some pretty hard looks. "This your nag?" he asked as I came up.

"It most certainly is."

"Where'd you get it?"

"Bought it in Seven Oaks a couple of days ago. Why?"

He eyed me some more. "Let's see your bill of sale, bub," and brushed back his coat to display a sheriff's badge pinned to his shirt.

I dug out the paper I had got from Evans. The sheriff studied it and then, much more searching, studied me. "Expect you must be new around here if you'd take Evans's word for anything. I'm taking it for granted you bought the horse in good faith, but I'm going to have to relieve you of it. This animal's the property of a man named Tunstall, stolen from him along with several others about a week ago."

I was pretty riled up. "This," I said angrily, "is the second stolen mount I've been relieved of in the past ten days. Don't you have any honest men in your baili-wick?"

"A few, son. Not many I'll grant you. You're talkin' to one now as it happens."

"Then where can I come by a horse that's not stol-en?"

That blue stare rummaged my face again. "You a limey?"

"If you mean do I hail from England, yes. I came here hoping to get to be a cowboy but nobody'll have me."

He nodded. "It's a hard life, son, an' considerably underpaid. Takes time to learn, but you seem young enough to have plenty of that. How much did you give for the two stolen horses?"

"One hundred and fifty dollars."

He considered me again. "You're pretty green, I guess. Most horses in these parts sell for forty dollars."

"A regular Johnny Raw," I said bitterly.

"Well . . . a mite gullible," the sheriff admitted. "Reckon time will cure that if you live long enough. Being caught with a stolen horse hereabouts is a hangin' offense. Come along," he said. "I'll get you a horse there's no question about, along with a bona fide set of papers to prove it. Do you have forty dollars?"

I told him I had and, counting out the required sum, handed it to him. He picked up the reins of Tunstall's horse, and we walked down the road to a public livery and feed corral. The sheriff told the man there what we wanted and the fellow fetched out a good-looking sorrel mare.

"This here's a mite better'n average, Sheriff—oughta fetch eighty. Trouble is these fool cowhands won't ride anythin' but geldin's. I guarantee this mare's a real goer. Try her out, boy. If you ain't satisfied, she's yours fer forty bucks."

The sheriff, meanwhile, had got my gear off Tunstall's horse. "Get me a lead shank," he said to the stableman. Transferring my saddle and bridle to the mare I swung onto her, did a few figure eights, put her into a lope, walked her around and proclaimed myself satisfied. The animal's name it seemed was Singlefoot. "She'll go all day at that rockin' chair gate," the man said. "Comfortable as two six-shooters in the same belt."

Thanking them both, I rode her over to the nearest café, tied her securely to the hitch pole in front of it and went in to put some food under my belt, pleased to see she looked very well alongside the tail-switchers already tied there.

Two

THE MURPHY-DOLAN STORE, I discovered, was by way of being a sort of hangout for one of the feuding factions. I met quite a number of interesting persons, chief among these being a chap who went by the name of Flick Farsom, best known as the man who had publicly declared he'd just as lief shoot Billy the Kid as any of the other McSween adherents. A marked man certainly, fast on the draw but friendly enough in a reserved sort of fashion. Asked about my chances of securing work at one of the roundabout ranches, he seemed something less than encouraging.

"Biggest drawback is your lack of experience. Best you could look for would be cook's helper. Bein' seen on a mare ain't much of a recommendation round here. Ain't much call for green hands nohow."

"Damn it, Flick. I've got my aim set on it. Counter hopping is all right I guess but not my style. I'm cut out to be a riding man."

He regarded me doubtfully. "If you're plumb set on it you better talk to the Major. He runs the cow end of this business."

I could see he wasn't much impressed with my appearance. Wiry, thin as a rail, I probably presented a kind of delicate look compared with the robust specimens who'd grown up around here. "Folks hereabout have you pegged for a limey—a butinsky. In your boots I'd make a dust for other parts."

He smiled at my scowl. "Of course, if you're set on bein' a cowpuncher, you could *habla* with Major Murphy. Or you could try to get on with Tunstall, which could be your best bet; he come over here from England. Money back of him, I expect. Has a spread not too far from here."

I can't seem to recall being filled with youth's belligerent certainties. I supposed he'd heard about me and those stolen horses. "Guess I could learn to cope," I muttered. In seventeen years I'd learned a good bit, but darn little of it seemed likely to help me here. Discovering how to conjugate a verb wasn't much of a shield against bullets, Flick said.

Until now anyway, being in a strange land—a foreigner really despite my birthplace—it had seemed to me an appearance of meekness was most befitting. It occurred to me now that an air of diffidence could be misconstrued.

We were back in the store when old Mrs. Potter came shuffling in. I was about to excuse myself to see what she wanted when the Dolan half of the partnership stepped up, all graciousness and unction. After she'd left with a spool of thread and two needles, Dolan came over like the wrath of God. "Didn't hire you," he said, "to stand gabbing with employees where there's customers to wait on! Go pick up your time and clear out."

"Are you saying I'm sacked?"

"I'm apt to say more'n that if you don't move lively. But I'll put it to you British style. This establishment can do without your services—savvy?"

Flick Farsom said, "That lady hadn't hardly come in when you showed up."

"When I need any yap from you I'll say so," Dolan said, looking ugly.

A kind of darkness came over Farsom's stiffening face, but he quit the store without further words. "Come along," Dolan said. "Back to the office and get your money."

I followed, thinking this summary dismissal was pretty high-handed but keeping a closed mouth. Opening a ledger, Dolan ran his eye over the figures and handed me half of what I figured I had coming.

"Where's the rest of it?" I said.

"The rest has been deducted for them oats your horse ate," he replied with a sneering regard. "You fixin' to argue about it?"

I leaned hard on my temper, took the money and departed, thinking this wasn't much like the West I had read about.

Major Murphy was on the porch lighting a cigar. Taking my courage in both hands, I accosted him. "Any chance, Major, of my catching on with the cow end of Murphy-Dolan?"

He puffed a few times with his stare running over me. "Thought you were clerking here?"

"Your partner just fired me."

"Not much of a recommendation is it?"

I met his look straightly. "I'd probably be more at home on the range, sir."

He said judicially, "Can't think of any place you'd fit in. Sorry." Then abruptly he turned back to ask, "Didn't I hear you were acquainted with The Kid?"

"He sold me a stolen horse."

"Well, there you are. Might be you'll manage to catch

on somewhere else," he remarked, and went into the store, smoke from his expensive cigar trailing after him. Doing my best to hide the seething inside me, I went around to the back to pick up my mare.

Seemed I was in the sort of fix that in these parts was known as being between a rock and a hard place. My finances were in a precarious shape. I could expect no further moneys from England until I could mail the solicitors an address where they could reach me, and I could see this was something I'd better do straightaway.

I rode along to a store that sold stoves and did double duty as a country post office. There I filled out my overseas letter, giving my direction as General Delivery, Lincoln, New Mexico. "How long do you imagine this will take to get over there?" I asked the bespectacled man behind the window.

"Ought to get there in three, four months I would think."

Chewing on that, I gave him the letter, paid the postage and went back to my horse.

Thinking about Dolan and the loss of my job, I thought perhaps a clash of personalities might well lie behind my discharge. The Irish hadn't much use for the British; it began to seem like no one in these parts had much love for them either. It was prejudice, of course; much the same thing that had got me sent down when I'd been going to school—a bullying headmaster and the lies of my peers. "It was Alfie, sir!" the culprits had cried. " 'Twas Alfie done it!" and I'd been sent home in unmerited disgrace.

And here it was happening all over again. There must be something wrong with me, I thought, something about my character or looks that aroused dislike in the persons who were in a position to help me. The only exception I could think of was the sheriff.

Having racked Singlefoot in front of the largest saloon, I went in and asked if there was work I could do. "If you ain't too proud," the bartender said, "you can have a job swamping." And this was how I came to be a sort of general dog's body, mopping out the place, emptying spittoons and otherwise making myself as useful as possible, even running occasional errands. Me, an earl's son!

At least it was honest work, though disgusting. To piece out my wages I was permitted to sleep in a kind of lean-to hitched onto the rear. The job certainly had no future. I took it to keep body and soul together until I was able to get money from home. Once my early work was done I was sometimes allowed to tend bar until noon.

Mostly I went unnoticed until one morning Jesse Evans came in. We considered each other in considerable surprise. Then Evans said, "Well! Never expected to run into you here."

And I said, figuring I'd nothing to lose, "Sold any more stolen horses lately?"

He stopped in mid-stride, the whole look of him darkening. "How's that?"

All that jovial bonhomie so frequently paraded had peeled from his face like sunburnt skin to reveal the ugliness beneath. I was feeling pretty ugly myself when I laid shooter and shell belt on the bar, stood leaning on my mop and eyeing him with all the bitterness in me. "Just wanted to know if you've sold any more stolen horses," I told him.

The long room got so ominously still I could hear the barkeep's cat scratching the door to be let in. "Why, you two-bit ass-end of nothing!" Evans said through clamped teeth and started for me, bunched knuckles bone white in that brittle quiet.

With a dexterous move, I put the filthy end of my sloshy mop smack into that murderous scowling countenance so hard it drove him staggering back, and while he was pawing at blinded eyes I let go of the mop and clipped him a beauty at the hinge of his jaw.

It threw him half-around. He was scrabbling for his iron when I kicked him in the crotch, and as he jack-knifed forward, I brought a knee up under his chin with all the furious hate that was in me.

He went back and down, out like a light.

The apron came bustling over to look at him. "Gawd!" he cried. "D'you know who that is?"

"Told me his name was Jesse Evans," and before I could catch enough breath to say more, the sheriff came pushing his way through the batwings. One startled look he gave the man on the floor; then he wheeled an astonished stare at me. "Get out of here, boy—real quick."

"Because I knocked down a horse thief?"

"You can't know what you're sayin'. That's Jesse Evans!" he said, shaking his head. "He's like to make you hard to find—"

"He's the one who sold me Tunstall's horse. If you're onto your job you'll take him in custody."

The sheriff looked taken aback. "You filin' charges?"

"Why not?" I said brashly. "Too many like him running loose round here."

The sheriff, stooping, relieved Evans of his hardware. Stooping again, he snapped the bracelets on him, and straightening, he said, "You're goin' to have to stick around for the trial you know."

"You take my advice," the barkeep said, "you'll dig for the tullies makin' far apart tracks. 'F he ever gits loose that heller will clobber you."

"If there's any justice in this county he'll be on his way to jail before I'm much older."

"You got more spunk than sense," the sheriff said grimly. "You sure as hell ought to be bored for the simples." He let out a gusty sigh. "Come along—I got to have your name on a paper."

I picked up my bucket and dashed the slops over Evans with considerable satisfaction, ignoring the shocked stares.

"You oughtn't to of done that," the apron told me with kind of a shudder.

When Evans was finally able to push himself up, he looked about as mean as a centipede with chilblains. We took him uptown and locked him in a cell. Back at his office the law at Lincoln lifted a sawed-off double-barreled shotgun from a locked case and put it on his desk with a box of shells. Pushing them toward me, he grumbled, "Just sign this complaint and you're free to go."

I still remember Sheriff Brady's kindness.

But thoughts of the hereafter began to gnaw into the satisfaction I'd felt at having worked off some of my spleen on Evans. The fellow was well known around these parts as a very tough customer, a gun-slinging hard case with a host of rough acquaintances; I don't say "friends" because his kind seldom have any. Right now Jesse Evans was on Major Murphy's payroll. So it seemed fairly probable he'd manage to get himself liberated. I'd just have to wait and see, I guessed. It might be just possible to keep him at bay with the shotgun Brady had given me.

I reckoned Brady was on the square. In his precarious

position it took a heap of guts to jug that bugger with a man like the Major looking over his shoulder. There had been a warrant for Evans's arrest floating round for a considerable while; the horse he'd sold me wasn't the first stolen critter to pass through his hands, according to local gossip. Evans, Frank Baker and others, it was rumored, had lifted several mules and horses belonging to Dick Brewer, Alex McSween and Tunstall, and been captured by Sheriff Brady and a posse near Seven Rivers on the Pecos. Locked in the jail that was holding Evans now, they'd been broken out by the rightful owners on Baker's promise to return the stolen animals.

Nothing further was known of the matter except by Brady, to whom I'd surrendered the stolen Tunstall horse Evans had sold me. I wondered if Tunstall would give me a job. Might seem strange to you, but I wasn't purely enthusiastic about depending on pay from an Englishman if that's what he was. The man was known to be a staunch supporter of the McSween faction that was hooked up with cattle baron Chisum, who was opposing Murphy-Dolan.

And that conscienceless Billy who had swindled me out of a hundred dollars was certainly on Tunstall's side of the fence.

True, Evans was now one of Murphy's understrappers. I couldn't like either of the pair who had robbed me, but of the two I guessed Evans to be the easier to get along with. He might have it in for me, but I did not reckon he would shoot me in the back. And Billy had laughed as he took my money.

It chafed me plenty to be played for a sucker.

Three

ANOTHER WEEK DRAGGED past with myself still pushing the mop in that grog shop and Evans still locked up in jail without intervention by Murphy. Began to seem like he was going to come up for trial if the court ever got around to sitting. With that bill of sale Jesse had signed I couldn't see how he was going to wriggle clear. But I was getting fed up with emptying spittoons. And doing it for a pittance.

Then one day it came to me Judge Bristol had given the sheriff orders to open up court and adjourn it, that he felt Lincoln was too unsettled at the moment. A fine kettle of fish!

Seemed like this Lincoln County feud was heating up more with each passing hour. I'd foolishly come here looking for action—the kind I'd got in my Wild West reading—but the way this thing was shaping up there looked apt to be more than I cared to contemplate. I was not at this point aching to be drawn into it.

Looking up the street through a fly-specked window, I said, "Thought the judge told Brady to get the court open and slam the door before anyone got in? What's he standing out there in the road for?"

The barkeep grinned. "Billy Mathews is the circuit court clerk and he ain't showed up—don't want to get daubed with the wrong end of the stick. Nor Dad Peppin ain't showed—both of 'em deppitys. Don't suppose Brady's too anxious to get turned into a colander either, but he's got guts all right. I wouldn't be in his boots for ten million dollars!

"Guess you ain't heard the Kid's sworn to blow Brady's head off account of that reward he put out with Billy's picture front an' center."

"You think Billy's here?"

"He ain't no loner an' there's a heap of bad actors loafin' round here right now. Little while ago he was over to McSween's place turnin' the pages an' caterwaulin' the hymns Mrs. M. was thumpin' out on Mrs. Fritz's pyanner."

I caught up my new shotgun. "Looks as though Brady could use a little help."

Aghast, the barkeep said, "You outa your mind?"

"Probably," I told him, stepping through the batwings into the hoof-deep dust of the road. Coming out of the bar's lampless gloom into the full smash of that New Mexican sun, it took me a couple moments getting my eyes to focus. Tramping up there, I took up a stand alongside the sheriff—seemed the least I could do for one who'd treated me right.

Brady threw me a grin. "No call for you to get yourself killed."

I managed to grin, too, though mine certainly wouldn't have grabbed any prizes. I said, "Where-at's this Billy that scares little children?"

"Don't know," the sheriff said, "but there come my deputies. Now I want you to get back out of the way. If you're bound an' determined to be a cowhand you look up Burt Mossman. He'll put you in the way of it." And he gripped my shoulder, gave it a squeeze and shoved me away.

Swinging round on a heel, deputies in tow, he struck off toward the courthouse, lugging his Winchester.

This town was populated mainly by Spanish-speaking people, a number of whom had their homes along this road, the well-to-do ones prudently hedging themselves behind surrounding adobe walls.

Staring after Brady and his reluctant deputies, I could see, of course, these whitewashed adobe shields, which were built chest high, but paid them little notice, all my attention being devoted to the sheriff. It was the judge and his self-serving tactics that mostly occupied my thinking.

This was a town where the laws, legislated by persons of Mexican and Spanish descent, had grown too lax. I suppose it wasn't so much the laws as the people picked to enforce them. Partiality and corruption may not have been confined to Lincoln, but it was plenty evident. Aside from Santa Fe, where the politicos and most of the state police hung out, the majesty of the law in New Mexico was spread pretty thin. To my mind Brady was an admirable exception, no more popular than a tax collector.

Being that it was the first day of April, you could look for pranks. So I was still still undecided, still gazing after him, when a racket of rifles ripped the roundabout quiet. The sheriff, throwing out both arms, let go of his Winchester, staggered and fell. A masterpiece of villainy, dry-gulched in broad daylight on the town's main street.

A dazzle of shifted metal drew my glance to the line of rifle barrels projected across a whitewashed wall.

I began to run. Too bitterly furious in the heat of this outrage for sober thought, I put every last ounce of my energy into trying to get up there before those killers could get away.

The three who'd been with Brady—Mathews, Peppin and Hindman—were likewise heating their axles, but the lousy cowards were running for cover. Hindman, seeming to have lost what little sense he'd ever had, was running straight toward me down the center of the road. Peppin and Mathews were scurrying for the protection of a Mexican's house just across the way. Three rifles atop the wall banged again—I could hear the reports through my panting, saw George Hindman stagger—it was like he'd been hit in the back with an axe.

Then I reached him, and across the wall I could see the retreating shapes of the assassins; saw French and Billy leap the far wall. Ike Stockton burst into the road, took a quick squint at Brady, yelled something out of the side of his mouth and was starting to run when I squeezed trigger. Saw him jerk, but he was too far away for that charge of buckshot to do more than pepper him. He kept right on going and rounded the wall out of sight.

Mrs. Captain Baca hurried into the road with a pitcher of water for the prostrate Hindman. She was shouting something after Billy, but he and his cronies were long out of earshot.

It was then, realizing Brady was dead, that I finally took stock of my own situation. Those cowardly killers had certainly seen me—they must have. For me to remain in these parts could be extremely unhealthy.

Quite a number of persons must have witnessed Brady's death; my own two cents' worth would not help anyone. I slipped round to the stable and got aboard my mare. I replaced the spent shell and, twisting round for a final look, saw French with a whoop snatch up Brady's rifle and that little bastard Billy crouch over the sheriff trying to tug off his shell belt just as Mathews, from the Mexican's house, got off a wild shot. The Kid jumped like a scorpion had got up his pants leg. French, howling, clapped a hand to his hip and went limping off.

I didn't wait to see more but lit a shuck out of there, bidding good-bye to Lincoln for what I hoped would be forever.

Later, mulling it over, considering the way the sheriff had treated me, I guessed I should have made a bigger push to avenge him. But uppermost in my mind at the time had been an urgent need to put every mile possible between myself and that bucktoothed Billy.

At Roswell I got a job at a livery, mucking out stalls and taking care of boarders. This was easily the best job I'd had but a far cry from being the dashing cowboy of my dreams. I recalled more than once Brady's parting advice, but I'd no idea where to find Burt Mossman. I did ask a couple of cowpunchers, but they peered at me blankly and shook their heads. For another two weeks I continued to clean stalls and care for the boarded horseflesh.

One afternoon a fiddle-footed cowhand came into the stable wanting to know how to get to Vaughn. Given directions by the proprietor, he didn't seem in much of a hurry to be on his way. Leaving his mount with us, he struck out afoot for the nearest saloon. He came back after supper, paid his bill and reclaimed his horse. While he was tightening the girth I spoke up to ask if he'd ever heard of Mossman.

He looked round at me sort of surprised and nodded. "Expect everyone in Arizona has heard of that waddy.

First captain of the Arizona Rangers, and a tougher ranny I never hope to see! Cleaned out the Hashknife, buried more outlaws than you could shake a stick at and scairt most of the rest plumb out of the country. Friend of yours, was he?"

"Never met him."

"What's he doin' these days?"

"Ranching, seems like. Someone said he might give me a ridin' job but I've no idea where to look for him."

"Sorry I can't help," the fellow said and, lifting a hand, departed.

The boss took me aside. "Look. I can see you're not best suited here. Hard for me to keep a feller who'll put in this time to good purpose like you've done. If you will stick with me I'll raise your wages—give you a dollar a day. Lot of cowhands don't make more'n that. What do you say?"

I wasn't much tempted, my heart being elsewhere, but I let him talk me into it with the promise of sending me along to Fort Sumner next time the cavalry auctioned off some mounts. Expect I should have been flattered by the trust reposed in me, a raw kid, but I was impatient in those days to get on with my life. A life on the open range is what I wanted. Those earliest dreams were still filling my head. I can tell you now that a man seldom knows when he's really well off.

It was another five weeks before the promised relief from boredom occurred. The boss said, "You pick me out some good ones but don't go over twenty dollars a head," and put a small sack of hard money in my hand.

It took me a couple of days to ride over there. Around the fort itself a small town had grown up. About the size of Lincoln, service people mostly and the liquor merchants who catered to them. A lot of troopers in the stores and bars hunting some deviltry they could set up after the fashion of soldiers everywhere. I expect I looked a pretty ripe pigeon.

One of these fellows said to me in a confidential manner, "If you'd care to get in on a good thing, cowboy, just pick up my trail when I move outa this place.

I gave him a superior smile, told him then I was here on business.

"You mean monkey business?" He gave me a wink. "I know where there's—"

"Not that kind of business. I'm here to see the commandant," I told this smart aleck loftily.

He looked duly impressed. "Yes, sir!" he declared, straightening himself to a ramrod stiffness. "Sergeant Haye will conduct you straight to him, sir."

All those *sirs* should have tipped me off, but I supposed they came with the territory, and followed the "sergeant" back into the barracks area, peering about with unconcealed interest. "This your first time inside the post, sir?" he asked in the friendliest manner imaginable.

I assured him this was true. "Very impressive," I said, to be courteous.

"It's that, all right." He put a hand on my arm. "We turn in here," he said, guiding me. And that's the last I remember till I found myself with a thumping head in the grip of a husky trooper with red hair and a freckled face who appeared to be helping me up off the floor.

I said stupidly, less than half-present, "What's this place?"

"Latrine, sir."

"Never mind brushing me off," I muttered. "Just tell me what I'm doing in here. This isn't the commandant's office, is it?"

"Oh, no, sir. I shouldn't think so."

I eyed him suspiciously. "How'd I get here?"

"Someone said you came in with the corporal."

"What corporal?"

"I've no idea—didn't see him myself."

I shoved a hand in my pocket and knew the worst. The sack of hard money was no longer there. I guessed I'd been pretty much of a fool, and the thought did nothing to regain what I'd lost. He may have seen the rage building up in me and made haste to excuse himself.

I was left with my bitter reflections.

Given time I might pay back the lost money. To return to the stable empty-handed would, in the light of previous jolts, probably land me in jail, and that was a notion I could not stomach.

So, once more, I found myself shifting scenery. Following the Rio Pecos I headed north, staying close to the river, well away from the road.

It took ten days to reach Santa Rosa, where I worked breaking horses for another ten days. Ample time to think more about Mossman, that ex–Arizona Ranger recommended to me by Sheriff Bill Brady as a possible employer. But I did not mention his name in Santa Rosa; I'd become sufficiently cagey not to do that. I had no desire to have any part of the past catching up with me.

I collected my pay and, quitting the Pecos, rode west to Palma, scarcely a fly speck on the map. Found no work for me there, and still moving west, I reached Moriarty and green-broke more horses for a small-spread rancher, still shying away from enquiries about Mossman. I can't think why I held off unless in some obscure fashion I imagined it would put a posse on my trail.

I did make a few guarded enquiries about prospects for work in Oklahoma, hoping to mislead any possible pursuit. I learned that Oklahoma was ranching country and, not overcrowded, was offering homesteads to ambitious persons with no aversion to hard work. Instead, I cut across to Las Lunas on the Rio Grande. And from there to Puerco, thence to Correo and, a month later, as far south as Quemado. And once more I hired out to break horses, the only sort of ranch job I'd been able to get.

Three weeks later, keeping away from much-used trails, I found myself in Arizona.

Broken Butte wasn't much of a town but was, at that time, well into the throes of a gold discovery and consequently booming. A true frenzy of excitement had laid hold of the inhabitants, each of them expecting to make a quick fortune, and prices for the very least of neccessities had jumped outrageously. Two dollars and a half for a slice of raw bacon and a badly fried egg, the first store-bought meal I'd had in two months.

While I was sampling my second cup of coffee I made some further enquiries. This too, it seemed, was ranching country, and along with the boisterous Anglos I saw plenty of mustached Mexican faces whose owners, like myself, had likely gravitated here from less desirable places. But most of these had the look of having been here some while, leading me to imagine I could forget about Lincoln and Roswell.

During the next few days I confidently expected to be employed by some "cow spread." With everyone caught up in this gold fever, I reckoned some of these ranches might be crying for help.

Gold, it appeared to me, must be something like an epidemic. It had certainly left its mark on these people. Looking round from my stool at the counter, I realized that I had seldom seen such animated countenances except at a bullring. Every table was crammed, but there was very little conversation, all seeming anxious to gulp down their food and get back to the "diggings" as fast as possible. Hard currency was very much in evidence along with gold dust and nuggets, and everyplace I went into had a prominent pair of scales and most usually presided over by a sort of hombre you'd not care to meet at the mouth of an alley. Hard, garish, excitable and rough is the best description I can give of Broken Butte.

I had left my mare, Singlefoot, in a stall at one of the three livery stables, paying a small fortune to have her properly cared for, thinking to get a better feel of the town mingling with the milling crowds thronging the rough plank walks. Mules and are wagons appeared to be in large supply. Busy was the word most apt for Broken Butte, cram-jammed with energy and obviously neck-deep in confidence, the babble of voices almost deafening.

That evening in another café I was lifting my cup when a mustached Mexican, joggling my elbow, caused me to spill the most of my fifty-cent-a-cup coffee across my shirtfront. He was a regular bull moose of a man. Not supposing this had been deliberate, I hung on to my temper, watching him brush on past to nab the only empty stool in the place. I gave the fellow no further attention beyond noticing that persons hurriedly moved away from his direction almost as if he were the carrier of some obnoxious disease.

Having paid for my meal, I cruised the boardwalks a while longer, finally stepping into what passed for a hotel in the hope of finding a room for the night. It became plain straightaway that I had walked into something.

Four

THREE MEN DOMINATED the cramped lobby.

The loutish grins on the pair nearest the counter directed my glance toward a taffy-haired girl furiously struggling to free herself from the grip of the third, which was when I spoke. I said, "Is that fellow bothering you, ma'am?"

The fellow who had the girl in his grip twisted his head to see who was fool enough to buy chips in his game. "Git!" he growled through a set of teeth that were yellow behind the drawn-back lips. "Hightail it!"

A burly, robust hombre, there was no doubt at all he was not of a mind to suffer interference. But, seeing the girl's distress, and being nowhere near as puny as I must have looked to this lecherous bully, I said, "Get your hands off that lady," much to the delight of his grinning cronies.

"G'wan, kid—beat it!" snarled this black-browed villain. "Clear out before I take you apart!" And he was about to resume his deviltry when I said to divert him, "You are welcome to try."

The pair of louts enjoying this byplay guffawed at my fighting stance. But their mouths dropped open when I fastened a grip on the back of his collar, yanked him loose of his white-faced victim and, as he spun round,

28

planted five knuckles at the hinge of his jaw. As he went reeling sideways, I discovered he was the rowdy who had spilled coffee over the front of my shirt. I poked him again for good measure.

The bruiser wasn't so much hurt as astounded.

Then with a roar, "Chihuahua!" he grunted, and came for me with a knife in his fist. I stepped back and caught him in the kneecap with the toe of my boot. As he doubled over, gasping, I lifted my own knee under his chin.

He lurched back against the wall, and before his feet were properly under him, I kicked him in the belly— hard. Air whooshed out of him, his eyes rolled up, the knife clattered on the floor and I gave him a facer that drew his cork. With the blood dribbling over his chin, he went down in a crumpled heap. I heard the girl gasp, and, giving her a grin, I rounded on the pair of oafs by the counter, who were staring at me with unbelieving eyes. I said, "Drag that carrion out of here before I throw him into the street."

When they continued to stare like a couple of deaf mutes I started for them with doubled fists. Both scuttled for the door and jostled themselves through it in a frenzied panic that did a lot for my self-esteem. With things going my way for a change, I dragged the groggy bully to the door, got him onto his wobbly legs and booted him through it, dusting my hands in the most approved fashion along the sides of my jeans.

The girl was eyeing me in a comical mixture of gratitude and horrified concern.

"Not to be alarmed," I said in my best swashbuckling manner. "I don't believe they'll be back. If you work here, miss, I'd appreciate a room."

She sort of shook herself together, green stare nervously rummaging my face. "That was El Miga you mopped up the floor with, the foreman of Armagón Posada, a cattle baron who owns more than half this county. I think you had better make haste to get out of here!"

"Why, I eat rowdies like him every morning for breakfast." I grinned. "I'd like a room, if you please. I feel the need to wash up."

She peered at me rather doubtfully. "Do you think you should?"

"Should what, ma'am?"

"Remain here."

I could see my presence was making her nervous. She cried, "El Miga won't forget this, you know," and sent a worried glance through the window. "And he always has three or four of the Posada crew with him . . ."

"Next time around," I said to impress her, "if he hasn't mended his manners I am liable to do him a harm. Now, about that room, miss—this *is* a hotel, isn't it?"

"Yes. My father, Nathaniel Higgins, owns it. I'm Dixie Higgins." Going back of the counter, she dredged up a key. "Room five," she said, "second floor," and pushed an open book toward me. "You'll have to sign." She produced a pen and an inkwell. "I think you should get right out of town—I honestly do."

With her taffy hair rather mussed by her tussle, she made, I thought, a rather fetching picture. Disregarding her alarm, I hauled the book toward me, still ensconced in the comfort of my prowess, and, dipping the pen, wrote, "The Last Chance Kid," and pushed the book back to her.

She called me as I headed for the stairs. "This won't do; we have to have a last name, you know, and either a first or your initials."

So, below my entry, I wrote, "Alfred Addlington, London, England."

"Are you British, Mr. Addlington?"

"Born in New York City," I said. "Any other statistics you feel I should add?"

She blushed, most becomingly. "I don't mean to be inquisitive. It's the law, you see. We are required to have a proper identification for overnight customers."

"That's all right. I don't mean to be offensive." I smiled. And this time when I started up the stairs, she let me go.

This was not my usual style with females. Actually I'm rather at a loss for words around them. I guess I was still a bit puffed up at having handled El Miga with such dispatch. I realize now it was mostly luck. He'd not been expecting so rude a demonstration from one he'd regarded as no more than a green kid.

Behind the locked door of number five I peeled off my shirt and swabbed the dust and sweat off me with water from the pitcher that sat in a bowl on top of the chest of drawers, and to prove to myself I was turning a new page in the history of Alfred Addlington, I even managed a shave. "The Last Chance Kid," I told myself with a grin, enormously liking the sound of it.

During my lonely and soul-searching travels after departing from Roswell I'd put in a deal of practice at getting my pistol out of its holster. I still lacked considerable of being a quick draw but reckoned in time I'd be bound to master the trick. If a man couldn't protect himself in this country, who else would care? With my knack for making enemies, there'd be times when that shotgun might not be handy, like now when I'd left it sheathed on my saddle.

Staying at a hotel seemed apt to swiftly diminish what money I still had, and I wished now I'd not been so hasty in giving the solicitors my direction, for I was not at all anxious to revisit Lincoln. Unless I could land a job mighty quick, I would soon be destitute. I guessed I had better get off another letter. But where else could I have my funds sent?

Moving around as I'd been lately, collecting my allowance could become a real problem. No telling where I'd be for the next several weeks. If it was going to take a whole month for a letter to reach London and still another before I could expect a reply, I was going to have to find a permanent address. And I thought again of Burt Mossman.

The nearest town of any size that I knew anything about was Roswell, and I could not like the notion of returning to Roswell until I could repay the money I had lost for that livery keeper. Also, near as I could calculate, Roswell was some two hundred miles from here. Lincoln was closer by about eighty miles.

I decided to put off writing for a bit. I could always write the Lincoln postmaster and have any accumulated Addlington mail sent on to me here I supposed. I got into my shirt, combed my hair and went down to the lobby.

The object of my gallantry was not in sight. Behind the counter when I stepped up was a slim and dapper gentleman who looked to be in his fifties. Peering through steel-rimmed spectacles, he said, "I expect you must be Mr. Addlington, sir. I must thank you for coming to my daughter's assistance. Most appreciated by us both, though I am sorry you became involved. A rude and arrogant outfit, those Posadas. I hope they don't make trouble for you."

Then Dixie appeared from a room behind the counter and added her thanks to her father's. "You're not planning, I hope, to remain here—" Catching the old gentleman's frown, she said, "I don't mean to sound ungrateful. It's just that . . ." She looked away for a moment. I thought to read despair in her look. "It's likely to make more trouble, I'm afraid."

"If you prefer that I leave—"

"But where would you go? There is no other hotel."

"There must be lodging of some sort. A room, perhaps, with some private family? I'll make out," I assured her.

Her father said, "It's this deplorable boom—everything's topsy-turvy. Please feel free to stay as long as you like."

I said, "I don't suppose you happen to know of a man called Mossman?"

"You mean Burt Mossman who was captain of the Rangers—old Cap Mossman?" asked Mr. Higgins, as if astonished.

"Do you know where I could find him?"

"As it happens I do. He owns the Turkey Track ranch south of Roswell and he's general manager of a cattle company that controls the Diamond A's. Has an office in the First National Bank building in Roswell. Are you an acquaintance?"

"Hardly that. I was told I might get a job with him." I gave them a smile, the biggest part of it for Dixie. "I'm obliged to you both." I lifted my hat and went out.

The plank walks were still crowded. There was no letup in traffic—ore wagons, spring wagons, buckboards and buggies in continual movement imposed a hazard to any pedestrian wishing to get to the road's farther side. This made for a seldom lifting fog of gray dust shot through with the hearty and frequently vulgar shouts of drivers.

I was standing on the porch trying to make up my mind if I should seek out Mossman when Dixie came out to put a hand on my arm. "Seriously," she said, "if I were you I'd not stay here a minute longer than was absolutely necessary. El Miga's not a man to trifle with, I assure you."

"Are you afraid I might do him a hurt?" I grinned.

Appearing exasperated, she went back inside.

Discovering his office, I visited the town marshal. Sizing him up for a reasonable man, I mentioned my run-in with Posada's foreman. "It seems the hotel keeper's daughter imagines this might make trouble for them."

The marshal nodded. "Posada holds a mortgage on the property."

"Is there anything I can do to relieve the situation?"

"Short of taking up the mortgage—buying it from Posada or giving Higgins the price to pay it off—I'd suggest you leave town till things simmer down."

Five

ONE WEEK LATER I rode into Roswell.

The First National Bank was not hard to find.

A lift took me up to the company's floor. A lady asked if she could help and I said I was hoping to speak with Burt Mossman. She said, "I am Miss Kelly, Mr. Mossman's secretary. If you'll excuse me I will go and find out if he can see you."

"Sheriff Brady at Lincoln advised me to speak with him about a possible riding job."

"We had heard Mr. Brady had been killed."

"That's right, ma'am. It was just prior to that when he advised me to come over here."

She went off and came back shortly to bid me follow her, leading the way into another office. "A young man to see you, Mr. Mossman. He tells me Sheriff Brady sent him."

The tall mustached man behind the desk leaned forward to grip my hand as Miss Kelly closed the door softly behind her.

"Took you a while to get here, didn't it?"

"Yes, well . . . I was there when they killed Bill Brady," I said, and gave him a short version of the affair.

He pushed a box of cigars across the desk and when I

declined, picked one out for himself and fired up. Through the smoke he continued to scrutinize me. "Don't believe I caught your name."

"Alfred Addlington, sir."

"Do I detect a British accent?"

"Probably. I was born in New York but educated in England. Father was English."

"What was his occupation?"

"Well . . . mostly he was concerned with horses. Rode to the hounds, kept a stable, attended race meets."

"Hmm. A gentleman then."

When I offered no comment, he kept eyeing me till I was forced to remark, "It was the general assumption."

This fetched me a sharp look. Then he asked abruptly, "What did you want to see me about, Addlington?"

"A job, sir—a riding job preferably. I have a mind set on becoming a cowboy. The sheriff seemed to feel you'd . . ."

"Yes, I see. Cowboying is a deal harder work than most of you young fellows imagine."

"Yes, sir." Watching him puff on his cigar I made bold to ask, "How long would it take me to learn?"

"I've no idea. Depends on a number of things. If you're quick to catch on and willing to apply yourself I expect you could get to be an average hand inside of a year or so. Tell me . . . why do you want to be a cowboy?"

"I can't honestly say. Just something that's sort of taken hold of me I guess. Mostly, perhaps, because it so aggravated my father, I suppose."

"Read a lot of cowboy stories, I expect?"

"All I could get my hands on, sir."

Mossman sighed. "If you're bound and determined I guess you'll be one. But there's a lot more to it than riding, shooting and raising hell. All that you can do without setting foot on a ranch, you know. Ranching is mostly grueling work and often pretty boring. Doesn't take a lot of brains to be a cowhand; in fact I've sometimes thought . . . Well, no matter. Dangling a six-shooter on your hip is a damn poor reason for saddling yourself with a life of hard work."

"Yes, sir. Point taken."

"If you work for me you stay out of trouble. One feud in this region is more than enough."

"Yes, sir."

He had the most penetrating stare I've ever encountered.

"Aside from wanting to be a cowboy, what other enticements sent you to the States?"

I could feel the heat climbing into my face. I twisted my hat around a few times.

"Youthful indiscretions?"

"You could call it that. And free transportation."

"Any girls involved?"

"No, sir. Pranks mostly. I was sent down from Eton. I did get into a couple of scrapes with the gentry." I took a fresh breath. "The truth, sir, is I was put on a boat, given an allowance and told not to darken the family doorstep again."

"A remittance man, eh?"

"Not of my choosing."

"They all say that," Mossman pointed out dryly. "Still, Bill Brady evidently thought well of you." He considered me some more. "I'll give you a note to the Turkey Track range boss. After that it'll be up to you."

And, picking up a pencil, he scrawled a few words on a scrap of paper and handed it to me, folded. "To save you looking, it says, 'This fellow wants to be a cowboy.

See what you can do with him. If he don't measure up
get rid of him.' "

"Thank you, sir. All I ask is a chance," I said.

Mossman nodded, told me how to find the Turkey
Track and was about to wave me away when I said,
"There's one other thing I expect you should know
about," and told him my story of the Last Chance livery
and my humiliating experience at Fort Sumner. "If you
could let me have an advance on my wages I'd like
to pay back that two hundred dollars before I leave
town."

He seemed to weigh me again. I thought he was about
to ask for the return of that note. He heaved another long
sigh and said, "Let's have that paper." When I handed it
over he wrote across the bottom, "Owes the Company
$200. Take it out of his wages."

My first job at Turkey Track was digging earth tanks
to catch and hold water. This was a bit more arduous
than it sounds. I dug three of them. Took me a matter of
three months before the boss declared himself satisfied.

He put me then to repairing windmills. This occupied me for another three weeks. I was then assigned a
string of seven company horses, most of them not quite
green broke. He said, "Two of these will be morning
horses, two for use in afternoon work. Two of the others
should shape up to be cutters and the other will be your
night horse.

He suggested which might be most satisfactory at
these various uses. But for the first three months of
my tenure at Turkey Track the only riding I did was
to and from the chores he found for me.

Next he put me to riding the bog holes, another piece
of grueling work. Then he put me to riding fence, a

mean and occasionally dangerous job. If the wire got loose from you while you were repairing a break, it could cut you in ribbons, into "doll rags" was the current expression.

By this time I'd picked up all I could of the local idiom, paying an eager attention when others were speaking. I did not hanker to be different; my greatest wish in those days was to belong, to be considered a part of the outfit. In school I'd acquired a considerable vocabulary that now I was doing my best to get rid of. In that day and place the use of "eight" and "ten-dollar" words to most of the folks I had anything to do with gave a less than favorable impression. Whenever I was able and had my wits about me, I endeavored to talk as the rest of them did. Cowboy lingo was a fascinating subject. I also put in a deal of practice at lifting my pistol out of its holster.

These various chores took care of most of my time for five long, and sometimes aggravating, months. I was not delegated to visit any ranches. "A stray man," the boss informed me, "is most generally a seasoned veteran— a top hand. And so far as possible this also applies to a roundup crew. But you're coming along fairly well, so next fall—if you're still around—you'll be on that crew."

The next chore he put me at was riding "sign," tracking down strayed cows. This, too, was a heap less easy than you'd think. One of the angles to this particular job was keeping them away from loco weeds, and likewise doing everything possible to protect my employer's interests. I soon discovered that frequently a strayed animal didn't leave enough tracks to trip up an ant.

Presently I became a wrangler, a job usually given a "button" or green hand. The wrangler who managed the remuda daytimes was called a wrangatang; the night herder was a night-hawk; and I was given a stint at both occupations. Being a night-hawk mainly consisted in keeping saddle horses from taking off on their own. When a crew needed horses these were expected to be at hand.

Fall came around finally and I landed the roundup chore of driving the hoodlum wagon. This was the wagon that carried the bedrolls and any extras the boss had no better place for. At this time I'd been working eight months for the Turkey Track without pay. As we got ready for the fall roundup, the boss, taking me aside, said, "You're not a finished cowhand yet but you're well on the way. Next month you'll start collectin' wages."

A mighty pleasing prospect as you may well imagine. Eight months with no pay was a sure-enough character-building stretch of time. I was eighteen now, considerably toughened up and a great deal more knowledgeable about the ranching industry than when I'd arrived, my skin the color of a well-worn boot.

I've neglected to mention my interview with the livery keeper whose money I'd so foolishly lost, which wasn't near as bad as I had thought it might be. He was in his late forties and a reasonable man.

He heard me out, grunted a few times and accepted the money Mossman had advanced me. Nothing was said about interest. I expect he was some tickled to get back his investment. Even said he'd be happy to take me back. I thanked him and explained that I was cowboying for Turkey Track. He shook hands and wished me luck in my chosen profession. Then he said, looking me over, "A man generally makes his own luck in this world. Behave yourself and you'll do fine."

With forty dollars coming for my next month's pay

I thought some of leaving once I'd collected it. I'd not yet come to fully appreciate the remarkable thing Burt Mossman had done for me. Still too young, I think now, to grasp the overall picture.

On some of my chores there'd been plenty of opportunity to practice getting my "iron" out of leather in a manner that appeared reasonably swift—not that I had any hankering to become a gunslinger. I think it was mainly a matter of personal satisfaction. Fortunately I'd done no bragging—hadn't once mentioned my efforts at attempting to become a quick draw. I did think I'd become fairly good at it, though, and as a consequence felt a deal more confident of my place in the community.

I even considered going back to Lincoln to claim any money being held at General Delivery. There'd been no way of keeping up with the feud down there. I'd heard Billy had been arrested and had escaped from the second floor of Murphy-Dolan's store, killing two men in the process.

Certainly I'd no wish to tangle with Billy, but I did want mightily to pocket any money the solicitors had mailed me. It seemed I'd developed a sort of restlessness generally attributed to barbers, an aching to discover what might be on the far side of distant hills. Two months later I bade goodbye to the Turkey Track, threw the hull on my private horse, Singlefoot, and headed south.

Lincoln looked about the same dusty cow town I'd left after Brady's killing.

No one hailed me as I rode up the dirt street between its twin rows of business establishments and the white-washed walls from which the sheriff had been ambushed.

I racked my mare before the stove store housing the

local post office and stepped inside to inquire about mail. I identified myself and asked if General Delivery was holding anything for me.

The man in the green eyeshade and cardboard sleeve protectors dug out seven registered overseas letters for me. "You're required to sign for each of these," he said, handing me a pen. Signing, I stuffed the thin envelopes inside my shirt, unopened, and buttoned my vest.

"How's the feud?" I asked.

"Two men killed yesterday. Did you know Dad Peppin? He's sheriff here now. Understand he's lookin' for deputies."

I wouldn't have served under him for three times the money, though I'd sense enough not to say so. I could still see him scurrying for cover the day they'd killed Bill Brady. "Well, thanks," I said. "Don't reckon I'm cut out to be a star packer."

Outside I got on my mare and singlefooted straight out of town, not even stopping to get myself a drink. If either of the factions remembered me, they might well have been keeping track of my mail. I'd had my fill of Lincoln.

I was still undecided about returning to Turkey Track. I did think perhaps I should at least pay my respects to Mossman; his giving me that chance had done a lot for me. In the months I had worked for his brand I had filled out more than I'd realized, and with seven registered letters inside my shirt, I felt like a different man.

But at Roswell Miss Kelly, after shaking my hand warmly, told me regretfully that her boss was out of town. "I think he's gone out to the Diamond A on company business. He'll be sorry to have missed you."

From there I went downstairs to the bank, produced my credentials and dug out the wilted envelopes from

England. Each contained a bank draft; none held correspondence.

I pushed all seven of them through the window. The clerk looked me over with no little astonishment. "Amounts to quite a sum of money," he declared. "May I see one of those envelopes?"

"Certainly. You may keep the lot," I nodded, sliding them under the grille.

"Bank notes all right?"

"Sure wouldn't care to cart that much in gold or silver."

He gave this a polite smile and counted out seventeen hundred and fifty dollars, which I thrust inside my shirt, shocking the poor sod again. "You'd be smart," he said, "to keep that in a belt."

"Don't have a money belt. Don't imagine I'll have it a great while anyhow," I said, and took my departure.

After so many payless months I felt like a sure-enough mogul. I stopped at the Chinese restaurant and treated myself to a fancy meal.

I still hadn't decided where to take myself next. I reckoned I ought to go back to the Turkey Track, but I was eighteen and a heap too reckless to know when I was well off. There were a pile of hills I hadn't crossed yet. It never once occurred to me to return to Broken Butte and my little feud with the Posadas' foreman.

In the end I struck out west once more, thinking I might give Tombstone a whirl. I had heard and read so much about that place, which was said to have a man for breakfast practically every morning.

I rode south to Alamogordo and through an edge of white sands into Las Cruces, and from there to Lordsburg, with a side hop to Shakespeare, where they'd just hanged Russian Bill from a dining-room rafter, and on through

Steins Pass and south once more to cross the "Sufferin Springs" Valley and, by way of Antelope Pass, into Pearce.

Thirty miles south and west was my current objective, a town founded on silver and still pretty woolly, the hell-roaring town of Tombstone, held at this time to be the largest around, a habitat I'd thought of innumerable times as I'd tailed angry steers from the Turkey Track bog holes.

Six

TOMBSTONE, BUILT ON silver in the very guts of the cattle country and, you might as well say, at the tag-end of nowhere, was a community of contrasts. Only a whoop and a holler from the Mexican border, it attracted the scum from both regions as sorghum attracts flies. It had its pockets of culture. Gourmet foods competing with hash houses. A whole section was devoted to soiled doves and other loose females who sold themselves cheap. Churches vied with gambling establishments. It had a quaint variety of law and lawmen, though most of the former were generally ignored. It was the hangout of rustlers, horse thieves and smugglers plus a considerable number of unclassified rogues.

Modern conveniences were interspersed with frontier trappings. Several newspapers flourished on a weekly basis. The Southern Pacific had recently built through town, the puffing of its engines adding to the general din. Asprawl at the moment in the splendid isolation of the tawny Sonoran desert, geared to round-the clock excitement, the town was more Wild West than even I, in my feverish dreams, had imagined.

Honest, hard-working persons rubbed shoulders with a considerable variety of arrogant desperadoes. Sixteen-mule ore wagons stirred clouds of dust as they rumbled through town day and night. There was a multitude of bright-wheeled buggies and fringe-topped surreys. Picturesque, hectic and deadly was the way I came to look upon Tombstone.

After a fortnight in residence I became so used to continual uproar I no longer noticed or gave any heed to it. A photographer with the unlikely name of C. S. Fly owned one of the many boardinghouses, and it was in his establishment on Allen Street not far from Bauer's butcher shop that I took up lodgings.

Not long after settling in I came out one morning to go pick up my mare and was hailed by a voice that seemed in some way familiar. Swinging round for a look, I discovered Flick Farsom heading my way at a good swinging stride, taking little account of the pedestrians between us. "Alfie," he cried, "imagine finding you here!"

"Quite natural." I grinned. "It's the hub of the universe!"

"Well, they like to think so anyway," he chuckled, shaking my hand like he'd hold of a pump handle. This was the man who'd publicly declared in Lincoln he'd as lief shoot Billy (that "damn little horse thief") as anyone else who was stringing their bets with the McSween-Chisum faction.

"Have you shot Billy yet?" I asked, reclaiming my hand.

"Not yet," Farsom said with his twisted grin, "but huntin' him is what's fetched me over here. I'm one of Dad Peppin's deputies now when I have time to work at it. How's tricks with you? You're lookin' good, Alfie."

"Feelin' good, too," I said, "up to a point. I been working for Mossman at Turkey Track."

"A sure-enough cowhand—damn if you ain't! Didn't

know ol' Burt had interests here—how is the old bastard?"

"Reckon he'll make it. I'm over here looking around for a good investment. Got a roll that's itching to quit my pocket."

Flick grinned, and I thought what a devil he must be with the ladies. "No problem there," he chuckled. "Town's full of rascals who'd be glad to relieve you, not only of a roll but every stitch on you. Wildest town I ever been in. You strike it rich someplace?"

"Well, not to say rich. What I've got is a little nest egg I'd like to put to work."

"This is a right lively place—never saw so many out-an'-out crooks in my life as they've got here walkin' the streets like they owned the burg."

"Glad to see you, Flick," I told him. "Can I buy you a drink?"

"Later. Right now I'm keepin' a sharp eye out for Billy." And he was off through the crowd with his big-roweled spurs and a wave of the hand.

Seeing Flick brought it all back, and I shook my head to get rid of those pictures it carried of Lincoln. We'd both had enough of each other I reckoned. I was looking for new horizons, and with unaccustomed wealth I'd stepped up to a larger outlook. As some fellow said, I was now in the land of opportunity, and I've got to admit I liked the feel of it.

A place like this could get into a man's blood. "Sky's the limit—if there is any limit," I told myself, grinning. Sure I felt good, plumb ready to take the bull by the horns.

And just about then Opportunity knocked.

A mustached fellow with string tie at throat sidled up to me with hand outstretched.

"Hi there, cowboy! How'd you like to get in on a sure thing? An unexpected crisis in the family is forcin' me to go back to Wisconsin; don't know when if ever I'll get back. Got a first-rate hotel I'm goin' to have to get shucked of—it's at Toughnut and Fifth, with restaurant attached. Back away from all this hullabaloo. Come along—won't cost you a nickel to see what I've got."

He looked honest enough and, like he said, no charge for the tour. So I followed along to have me a look. On the lefthand side, with a proprietor's delight, he pointed out the property. Its name was the Russ House.

Not exactly imposing, but spruced up with paint, it had a good solid look that if not ostentatious appeared respectable. "Had several nibbles," this old boy declared, "but I've no time to fool around—ought to've pulled out yesterday. Step inside and you'll have a better idea of what I'm goin' to have to give up."

The place was shuttered and obviously closed. "Had every room filled," he said, "but had to turn 'em out when I got that wire day before yesterday." He fished in a vest pocket and brought out a key, put it into the lock and threw open the door.

"After you," he said, stepping aside.

We spent the next thirty minutes going over the place, room by room. It was in good condition, much better than I'd expected, and much better furnished than my own room at Fly's. Neat and shipshape, almost dust-free, which, in a town like Tombstone, was saying a great deal, with all those ore wagons churning up the air.

"How'd you happen to single out me?"

"Somethin' smart-lookin' about you—I don't know. You looked prosperous, I guess. What do you think of it?"

"Don't look half-bad. What price are you after?"

"Well . . . like I've said, I got to get out of here, no time for backin' and fillin'. I figger by your looks you been punchin' cows—probably ain't too flush at the moment. Minute I seen you I said to myself, 'Cashman,' I said, 'yonder's a chap who has come into money—got the hard cash look.' How about it. Lay you odds I'm right. Sized you up for a gent who'd know a good thing when he saw it. Place is a reg'lar bonanza an' I hate like sin to let loose of it, but"—he threw up his hands—"for a quick turnover—cash in hand—you can own this establishment for one thousand clams."

I could hardly believe my ears. "What's wrong with it?"

"Not a thing. Duty calls and I can't fool around." He said, pretty earnest, "What I'm asking ain't a drop in the bucket to what they're gettin' for real estate here in Tombstone right now. Even vacant lots if you can find one. Go down to the bank an' ask what the Russ House is worth."

We talked for pretty near an hour I guess, and I could tell he was getting in a sweat to be gone. It finally wound up with me buying the place. It gave me a fine important feeling, looking it all over again after he'd left, knowing myself the proprietor of a going concern. I'd paid him the money and got a receipt, and with a final handshake Mr. Cashman left, leaving me lord of all I surveyed.

This change in my fortunes took a bit of getting used to. As a man of property in an up-and-coming metropolis, as you might say, I took a deal of interest in my first business venture, found a number of things the laws required me to see to. Licenses and permits. A staff to be hired, with good cooks scarcer than hen's teeth. In fact I spent ten days just trying to find a sign painter.

In the course of my inquiries I thought some of these folks gave me rather odd looks, but I put this down to being what was called a "foreigner"—foreign to them anyway. I was figuring to change the hotel's name till Flick took me in hand. "Why waste your loot? What's the matter with the name it's got?"

"Doesn't the Hotel Addlington sound more posh?"

"Be throwin' away a name that's recognized for one that ain't," Farsom said. "Can't see much profit in that."

Put that way I guessed I couldn't either. So I left the old sign just as it was. "Say," Flick said as he was about to depart, "you hear about Curly Bill? Earp killed him; leastways that's what they're saying."

I said, not much interested, "Who found the body?"

"Well . . . that's the nub of the matter. Seems they ain't got no corpus. Everyone's augerin' about it. Half of them's askin' where-at's the body and nobody seems to have any idea."

"Who says Earp killed him?"

"Says so hisself," Farsom grunted. Then plainly puzzled he asked. "Why say he did if he didn't?"

"What did he kill him for?"

"Never thought to ask. They been squawbblin' back an' forth quite a spell is what I've heard—no love lost between 'em."

Not terribly interested in either Curly Bill or that star-packing Earp but not wanting to appear indifferent to a matter the whole town found cause for speculation, I said, "If he killed him there's got to be a body. How's it happen no one has seen it?"

"Didn't happen in town, from what I hear—out with the hoot owls someplace."

"No skin off my nose," I told Flick. "What I'd like to find is an experienced cook—preferably a chef for the restaurant part of my new venture."

"Wish you luck," Flick said, pulling open the door. "I'd think what you'd need before anythin' else is customers," he added, and went off whistling "The Cowboy's Lament."

Until I could get hold of a cook there wasn't much use opening up the restaurant. I did have the hotel's front door repainted, a kind of heavenly blue, which I figured went well with the flashy brass doorknob. I hired a man in a rented monkey suit to open and shut it for customers, to give a bit of swank to the Russ House. After paying him wages for a solid week, the only outside person to approach the premises was a beaten-up drunk with a knife-split cheek who was hunting the female who sewed up casualties.

When the doorman called me I sent the drunk over to see Dr. Ritter. It wasn't until two weeks later that the sky started to fall.

Seven

WHEN HE WASN'T hunting Billy, my Lincoln friend Flick Farsom was a big help in getting me settled in. He was a real fix-it man, a jack of all trades it seemed like; good at scrubbing and painting and carpentry too and, eventually, a stand-in for me when I wasn't available. In return for which I gave him free lodging. I once told him wistfully if he could find me a cook he could figure on getting free meals besides. Cooks around Tombstone were in short supply.

I'd given up my room at Fly's boardinghouse and moved into the hotel. But one bright morning Fly came by with his tripod to make a picture of myself and the staff beneath the sign in front of the entrance. Flick, on tap, appeared somewhat dubious when Fly ducked under his black cloth to make sure of his focus, and Flick's anxious look showed in the finished product. But the doorman and I looked happy as two clams. Fly made us an enlargement and this we hung over the reception counter.

At the beginning of my second week as a hotel keeper we began to get a little custom. With five rooms taken I regarded my future as assured and was satisfied I had found my life's work.

It was that very afternoon that Josephina turned up.

Behind the desk, teetered back in my handsome swivel chair, regarding her with astonishment and a faint feeling of disquiet, I informed her that the Russ House did not cater to gypsies, at which she reared up like a prodded scorpion.

"Ha!" she cried, black eyes flashing. "What is this gypsies stuff? I'll have you know I am descended from kings! Do not geef me that evil eye, Mister Last Chance Keed!" and she stamped a foot like a flamenco dancer with an imperious look of outraged dignity.

"I'm sorry," I said. "There are no rooms available."

"Ho! Then you make one available!"

Irascibly I wiped the sweat off my brow. "If you leave peaceably you'll not have to be thrown out."

Like claws her furious stare raked my features. "You theenk I can't pay? *Cuidado, hombre!*" Yanking a small sweat-stained sack from between her breasts, she flung it onto the counter like whoever it was scattered pearls before swine. "Stand up like a man and have a look at this, *gringo*!"

I picked up the sack and shook some of its contents into my hand. "Those are gold nuggets," she said with curled lip as if I couldn't tell gold from rabbit pellets. "Now book me a room—*andele, pronto*!"

I refilled the sack and eyed her some more. She was not real big except in the chest, maybe five and a half feet from that mane of black hair to her open-toed *huaraches*, but she had a big voice that might well have been heard all through the house. She was as shapely a bundle as you'd be likely to find and right now, with her hackles up, more than just pretty. Lips red as a rooster's comb. And how had she known the name I'd written into the register at Broken Butte?

She didn't look more than seventeen or eighteen in her bedraggled gypsy finery, bare-legged and belligerent. She couldn't have topped the scales at more than six stone soaking wet. I'd a very strong hunch no more than she'd stepped through the door that here was trouble with a capital T.

"I am called Josephina," she informed me. "I am not one to take no for an answer. And I can speak the English as good as you when I am not . . . ah . . . excited. You give me a room or I make a horrid commotion in thees place. You have my gold. I demand a room. *Sabe?*"

I could picture her running to the sheriff claiming the Last Chance Kid had taken her gold and refused her a room at the Russ House. I wished Flick Farsom was not off hunting Billy.

But wishing would not oil any six-shooters.

With a bitter sigh I pushed the book toward her. "Write your name and home address as required by the law—the *whole* name, if you please."

A satisfied grin curled her gamine's mouth. Dipping pen into ink, she made a quick scribble. Hauling the book around, I read: Josephina Maria Vaca y Toro, El Paso, Texas. I glared at her. "Cow and Bull is not a name—"

"It," she declared all huffy again, "ees the name I was born with. The key—quick, or I will make you sorry."

I stamped hard on my temper. "I'm sorry already," I said, and dropped a key on the counter. "You pay," I said, eyeing her sack, which she hadn't picked up, "in advance."

She stuck her tongue out at me, grabbed up her little sack and flew up the stairs at a gallop, grinning back from the landing. I pretty near swore but controlled myself. "Room seven," I called, "fifth door on the right," and was turning away when a hopeful thought struck me. "Where is your luggage?"

"It will be here." Making another face at me, she flounced off out of sight.

Later, thinking of those nuggets, it occurred to me she might actually have panned them out of some stream. This might account for the brush-clawed look of what she'd had on. Nearest stream to El Paso, far as I knew, was the muddy Rio Grande, and these nuggets had never come out of that! They could have come out of Mexico, but to me the most likely source, all things considered, almost had to be some stream in the vicinity of Broken Butte. This was an oddly disquieting conviction. I couldn't help wondering how much the Posadas had to do with Josephina . . . Had they sent her? Was she a Posada? She most certainly was not the offspring of a cow and a bull!

Nor could I believe her someone who had merely chanced to wander into the Russ House, of which I was the latest proprietor. There had to be some connection between this fascinating enigma and the gold camp of Broken Butte. I could see no way round such an assumption. I wondered uneasily if she were related to the lecherous El Miga whom I could readily believe had not forgotten me.

In a place like Tombstone a personality such as hers could hardly fail to herald trouble. Briefly I thought of having Farsom arrest her before I recalled he'd no authority here, being clean out of his bailiwick. I had no grounds for her arrest by anyone. I guessed I'd just have to wait and try to discover what she was up to.

And it suddenly came over me I'd just as lief Farsom with his come-hither looks and brash assurance remained ignorant of her presence, and could see at once this was highly unlikely. He was bound to get a look at her. And equally bound to attract her interest. I might regret having given him a room here, but how could I turn him out of it now? I could not believe he would go if I asked him. I did considerable swearing under my breath. I wasn't even sure I wanted *her* to go.

The next time I saw her she was dressed to kill as they said in these parts. She had her black hair put up in the Spanish fashion and a devil in the sidelong glance she flung me.

I pretended not to notice, wondering where she'd got hold of the glad rags. She threw up her chin and, in a grand lady fashion not even London could have bettered, primly settled herself on the lobby's horsehair sofa in full view of the door. I could cheerfully have throttled her.

Flick, coming in a short time later, took one look and froze in his tracks, ogling her with obvious approval. It was her turn now to pretend she hadn't noticed.

Farsom, crossing the lobby, took up a lounging stance against the counter. Bending his head, he lowered his voice, but not quite enough to keep her from hearing. "Where'd you catch hold of that one?"

"Keep your mouth shut, you fool. She's a guest of the hotel."

"Must have money to burn by the looks of that outfit. Where'd she come from?" He pulled round the book and read off her name. "A real sense of humor," he declared with a wink. "Nothin' like that ever come from El Paso."

"Would you believe Broken Butte?"

Flick raised his brows, his look subtly changing.

"Within two minutes of coming into this place she called me the Last Chance Kid, which was how I signed into a hotel up there. What do you reckon she's up to?"

"Leave it to me, pard—I'll find out," he muttered, stepping away from the counter, and he approached the girl, whipping off his black hat with a swashbuckling flourish. "Flick Farsom, ma'am, at your service," he said with his most engaging twist of the mouth.

She looked stonily past him, and Flick said, "Don't I know you from somewhere? Perhaps you've forgotten. I'd swear we've met—couldn't forget a face like yours, ma'am. Kind to launch a thousand ships! Sure you don't recollect me? Must've been up around Broken Butte—"

Her look grew more haughty. She said, with her chin up, looking square at me, "I demand that you remove this person from your lobby."

"Afraid I can't hardly do that, ma'am. He's a guest here same as yourself."

With a nasty look, she swept to her feet and went up the stairs with not another word.

Farsom chuckled. "Real class there!"

"What do you reckon she's up to?" I asked.

"Don't know. Could be most anything. She was not trying to make my acquaintance, that's for sure."

I had told him about my run-in with El Miga. "You reckon she's related some way to those Posadas?"

Farsom grinned. "Plenty arrogant enough. Powerful easy on the eyes." He said with his easy assurance, "I'll find out—"

"You keep away from her."

He looked me over, plainly amused. "Reckon you've growed up some since Lincoln. Don't trade on it, Alfie. Wouldn't want you to git hurt."

I could feel the heat rushing up from my collar. He patted my shoulder. "Don't worry—I'll take care of her."

He was heading for his room when I growled at him bitterly, "I just don't want any trouble is all."

"No trouble." He grinned and went off with a laugh, leaving me to stew in my own juice so to speak.

Riled though I was, crammed to the teeth with resentment, no one had to warn me I was no match for him.

After he'd left she came back down the stairs and, shaking out her skirts, resumed her regal place on the sofa. I tried to ignore her, but the cards were against me.

I finally came out from behind the counter, walking grimly over to stand square in front of her. "Are you trying to attract attention?"

After considering me awhile she remarked in that husky voice of hers, "I don't have to try, señor," and gave me one of her brazen smiles.

I could see I'd not get much change out of her. But I went on with it anyway. "Are you related to the Posadas?"

A tiny laugh tinkled out of her. "Did that gringo oaf put that in your *cabeza*?"

"That 'oaf,' " I said, "is a deputy sheriff!"

"Is he going to put me in the calaboose?"

She looked so amused I told her abrasively, "You've not answered my question."

"My memory is not of the best today. What was it you asked?"

I knew she was mocking me. But I said again, "Are you related to the Posadas?"

This fetched back her gamine grin, and she twinkled. "I never thought to ask."

"Then what are you doing here?"

That devilish look returned to her features. "You'll never believe it."

"Try me."

She said with her eyes looking straight into mine, "I came here to look at you."

Eight

NOT MANY, I'D imagine, are prepared for such devastating frankness. I expect I stared in open-mouthed astonishment. "You came," I said when I got back my voice, "to look at *me*? Whatever for?"

The gamine grin crossed red lips with a chuckle. "But of course."

I found the directness of her regard disconcerting. I felt sure this was some sort of game she was playing, some deviousness I just couldn't grasp. I had never encountered her like in this country; in Chelsea, of course, among female artists and other loose women, I assumed her counterpart could be found, but I'd not numbered one among my acquaintance. She had me off balance, and I could see that she knew this and probably relished it.

I was furious, and guessed she could see that, too.

"I'm here of my own accord," she remarked as though reading my mind. "Did you imagine I'd come so far for a laugh?"

Whatever she'd come for, it seemed pretty certain she was getting her money's worth. The mockery was gone from her stare when she said, "I have the great curiosity to look at the boy who could whip El Miga with his bare hands—you are surprised? Nothing like this ever happened before. Everyone spoke of it and there was much pleasure at El Miga's discomfort. And Amargón Posada—that great tub of lard—was so incensed he have El Miga chased off his ranch. He did not wish such an object of ridicule associated with his name."

I stared incredibly. "You'd spend all this time and gold just—"

"The gold is nothing. I have a small mine. But such a boy, I tell myself, must be truly unique! You must know" —she grinned—"what happened to the cat . . . the one that looked at the king?"

The tinkly laugh burst out of her again. "I've a demon inside. It is very impulsive."

I was not to be sidetracked, but couldn't resist asking, "Why do you use that fetching accent so seldom?"

This brought out her dimples. "You 'ave notice?" She laughed. "I told you; sometimes when I'm upset or provoked I forget my high estate and words rush out too fast for me to catch them. It . . ." she said with that quick gamine chuckle, "it is the peon influence."

"You should cultivate it."

Whoever she was, wherever she'd come from, I became resentfully aware I was spending too much of my time on her and probably piling up trouble between myself and Flick Farsom, who seemed much too much taken with her. For my peace of mind, that is, though why I should care was completely beyond me.

Trying to rid my mind of her, I did some more thinking about that empty and unproductive restaurant collecting dust at the back of this establishment, an eating place that had—according to several of the guests—been greatly popular for miles around. And Farsom, just then, came back from his room at the end of the hall. In his brash fashion he muttered, "Ask if she can cook."

Her chin came up. "Of course I can cook! What girl—"

"Never mind the chatter. Could you dish up a meal for fifty persons?"

"But of course—why not? And what has that to do with anything?"

"I've a restaurant that's been closed since I bought this place. I haven't been able to find a decent cook."

"And where is this? I am permitted to see?"

"You bet," Flick said, taking hold of her arm. "Right this way," he said, and led her off down the hall, with me tagging along to watch her examining the room with much interest.

"And the kitchens?" she asked me over his shoulder.

"Back here," Flick said, steering her along for a look. "I'll give odds Spanish cooking oughta make quite a hit."

He was doing his best, I could see, to shove me into this, willy-nilly, anxious no doubt to keep her on tap. Just the same it was a thought I pursued in spite of misgivings. If she really could cook and was willing to do it, I reckoned she might prove a considerable attraction. "Hey, Alfie! What do you say?" he asked with his eyes about to gulp her down whole. "She could double your profit!"

I saw her eyes twinkle as they came back to me. "And what would thees Last Chance Keed do for me if I should make his restaurant the talk of the town?"

I said with a nag of reluctance I couldn't really account for, "What would you want?"

"Let us try this out for a month," she suggested. "If I keep the place filled . . . then we talk about price, eh?"

"Done," I growled, and shook her hand on it, reluctant, until I saw her amusement, to let the hand go. She made me feel like a fool, and it pretty near changed my mind then and there.

At Flick's suggestion she decided we would call the place Old Spain, and I had it done over with much advice from Josephina to give it, she said, a true Spanish flavor. It became a howling success no more than it was opened. Every room in the hotel became filled overnight and with, moreover, a considerable waiting list.

I was sitting on top of the world. But that uneasy feeling kept building inside me. And the better we became acquainted, she and I, the deeper that disquiet dug into me. A premonition I could not account for.

Three weeks after she became the celebrated "chef" of the Old Spain restaurant, a man who said his name was Pascholy stepped in one day to have a few words with me. I took him into my office, and since he was well dressed and had a businesslike air, I waved him into a chair and pushed a box of cigars across to him. "What can I do for you?"

I was still in my jeans and cowboy boots, and though I'd removed the spurs, I had on a bright shirt decorated with embroidered flowers some squaw had made for me. He had already looked me over outside. Now he eyed me some more. Then he said with a smile that looked cold as a well chain, "I'd like to know when and by what means you acquired this place."

"No secret about it. I bought the Russ House and restaurant about six weeks ago from the former owner, a fellow named Cashman."

Smooth as silk he said, "There ain't no such critter."

I don't deny that gave me a jolt. But as a man of substance I put on a bleak smile. "Afraid you're mistaken. I saw Cashman, talked with him, put the money in his hand right in this very room, Pascholy. He'd fetched the key from his pocket and opened the place up to show me around."

"And sold you a bargain, I'll warrant."

"I have the deed," I told him.

"A forgery, sir, as I intend to prove. What reason did he advance for disposing of so valuable a property?"

"A crisis in the family. Seemed to be in a great sweat to get back to Wisconsin."

"To get out of town at any rate," Pascholy said dryly. "It may interest you to know I'm part owner of this property. My associate, Miss Nelly Cashman, and myself have been out of town these last couple months. You can imagine my astonishment when I got off the stage this morning to discover we'd sold the property. Sheriff Behan will be along shortly to verify what I'm telling you."

I stared at him numbly. I was horrified, scarcely able to take in the magnitude of this disaster.

"Sorry you've been victimized," Pascholy said, "but I reckon you'll have to pack up and leave." And just as he was saying this Sheriff Johnny Behan stepped into the office, and Pascholy said, "Better show us that deed, Addlington."

I dug it out of a desk drawer and handed it over, both men inspecting it. Behan said, "That's not Miss Cashman's signature—nothing like it. What did this feller look like?"

When I'd described him, Pascholy said, "Sounds like Pete Spence," and the sheriff nodded. "A small-time grifter and tinhorn gambler."

I muttered in a daze, "When do you want us out of here?"

"Well," Pascholy said, "I don't want to be too hard on you for I can see you've put in a lot of improvements, but if you're out by tomorrow that will suit me fine."

Nine

FARSOM AND I picked up our belongings along with the cash I had taken in and quit the Russ House directly after we'd had our supper. Flick dropped a consoling hand on my shoulder. "Pretty rough on you, Alfie, but look at it this way. You just weren't cut out for this sort of business. Too confinin'. Gent like you has to have some elbow room."

I was in no mood to be cheered up. I felt like a first-class ninny. I bought me a bottle and went back to my old room at Fly's, locked the door and in the next hour and a half consumed the whole quart and was out like the lamp I hadn't even thought to light.

Josephina came around in the morning to commiserate with me. I expect I was scarcely civil. I do recall her saying she had turned down an offer from Pascholy to keep her on as cook. But she'd kept the room she'd paid such a large advance on, and Pascholy had agreed to this in the hope she might change her mind and go to work for him. "Perhaps," she offered brightly, "if we put together your money and mine we could buy another eating place and give that bugger a run for his money. I'll bet we could keep nearly all of our customers. Flick's taken down all the drapes and decorations; I've got them up in my room."

But I was too deep sunk to show any interest, and she finally left.

That afternoon, hearing that Wells-Fargo had been having an epidemic of stage robberies, I set out for their office on Allen Street, and just as I got there a coach from the OK Corral drove up, stopping in front. The driver jumped down and strode into the office and came staggering out under a heavy green chest with four or five passengers following him.

With everything loaded, including a crate of chickens, which was put on the roof, the driver climbed to the box and shook out his whip. Three teams of matched horses lunged into their collars, and off they went with sundry rattles and thumps. With the dust boiling up I thought I might like to try my hand at a job that required no brains, only risk.

When I stepped inside a clerk in sleeve guards and a green eyeshade looked up from his waybills. I asked for the manager.

"That'll be the agent, Marshall Williams," I was told. "Go left down that hall, second door to the right."

Since the door was open I stepped right in. A man in his forties with a genial face rose from his desk to look me over. "If you have a complaint take it up with the clerk."

"No complaint. I'm here about a job."

"Well, that's news," he said, inspecting me again with a deal more interest. "You any good with a shotgun— I could use another messenger. Got a stage going to Benson first thing in the morning. What's your name— had any experience?"

"Name's Addlington. I've been running a hotel. Before that I rode for Cap Mossman."

"Diamond A?"

"Turkey Track."

"How is the old mosshorn?"

"Pretty chipper."

"What was your occupation before you met up with Burt?"

"Bronc stomper."

He seemed to be eyeing my fancy shirt. "You ever been in a shootin' scrape?"

"I was in Lincoln when they shot Sheriff Brady."

He took a while to chew over the neat way I'd put that, glanced at my hip and up into my face. "How long did you work for Cap?" he said finally.

"Nine or ten months—I wasn't fired if that's what you're getting at. I reckon you can check that out pretty easy."

The agent nodded. He glanced again at my hip. "Generally hit what you aim at?"

"Generally."

"Ever use a shotgun?"

"I've handled one."

He seemed to be weighing me some more. Abruptly he said, "It's only fair to say ridin' shotgun around these parts ain't the healthiest job a man could get into. If you still want the job and you're here first thing in the morning you've got it."

I nodded. "Haven't seen Pete Spence around, have you?"

"Last I heard he was over at Galeyville." He looked at me sourly. "An acquaintance with Spence is a damn poor recommendation for a job with Wells-Fargo."

"The acquaintance was brief. I'm looking to put a flea in his ear."

Bright and early next morning I was back at the stage office. Having tied my mare to the hitch rail, I was heading for the office when I stopped, stiff and staring at the familiar hulking big-hatted shape lounging against the counter. His head twisted round to see who had come in. For the split part of a second he stood as stiffened as I was.

Neither one of us said anything. When his hand streaked for leather the sound of my shot in those close confines was pretty near deafening. The hulk, thrown off balance, slammed into the counter and, sagging like a ripped bag full of oats, slid down the pine boards as the knees folded under him.

The white-cheeked clerk with his eyes big as saucers cried, "My Gawd—you've killed him!" as Marshall Williams came running into the room. His glance jumped to the smoking pistol in my fist. "What happened?" he demanded with a swiveled look at his clerk.

"That feller," the man said, pointing a shaking hand at the heap on the floor, "was tryin' to get out his gun when this feller shot him—fastest thing I ever seen!"

Williams said, "Go fetch Behan. Tell him we've got a dead man here and I don't want this cadaver scarin' off customers."

As the clerk ran off, Williams chanced a look at me. "You got anything to say?"

"Guess your clerk said it all."

Williams stared some more. "That your mare outside?"

When I nodded, trying to keep the shakes from showing, the agent said, "Get your saddle off and leave her in the corral out back, then come in here and wait for the sheriff. You're hired. Get yourself a sawed-off from that case in the hall. You'll be leavin' on the Benson stage in"—he looked at his watch—"just about ten minutes."

Time I'd put Singlefoot in the corral and put up the bars, Sheriff Behan in his bowler was standing there looking me over, the stump of a cigar jutting out of his face. "You know who that was?"

I nodded. "Fellow called El Miga, *segundo* to the Posadas up at Broken Butte."

"You do get around," Behan remarked, pretty dry-like. He rolled the stogie across the crack of his mouth. "All right," he growled, "you're free to go."

Outside the office a couple of men were loading El Miga into the bed of a wagon. As they went off with him the stage rolled up, and I climbed aboard with the double-barreled shotgun Williams had handed me as the driver came out with the strongbox under one arm and the mail sack over his shoulder. "If you get held up," Williams called, "shoot to kill."

The driver shook out his whip over the backs of the leaders, and we were off, hellity-larrup, heading north in a cloud of ballooning dust.

"You ridden messenger before?" the old driver asked through a mouth filled with chewing tobacco.

"First time."

"Main thing is don't let yourself git rattled, son. We git held up I don't figger to stop. Just hang on to that Greener an' blast hell outa them. Fer cripes sake don't hesitate or it'll be us that gits blasted."

"Yeah," I said, still thinking about El Miga.

"These road agents is gittin' thicker'n flies round a sorghum barrel. Killed two of our messengers last week, one of 'em with his hands up."

I was beginning to wonder what I'd let myself in for. I was hoping I wouldn't have to do any shooting, but win or lose I was stuck with it now.

Everything went fine as silk for a number of miles and we had just about reached the halfway mark when

"Stand an' deliver!" came a shout from the brush off to the left and a slug whined between my head and the driver's. I could hear his whip pop and snatched up my Greener, tripping both triggers without a thing coming out of it—not even a bang. I let go of it and yanked out my six-shooter as a pair of masked robbers ran into the road. I squeezed off three shots as the horses lunged past. As we went pounding up the slope of a hill, the old man said with considerable approval, "Nice work—you got 'em both!"

When the grade leveled out he yelled, "What happened to that shotgun?"

"Don't know," I yelled back over the racket of the wheels as we rattled through the ruts. Grabbing it up, I broke it open, saw the shells in the breach and both of them dented. "Reckon somebody must've tampered with these shells."

The driver, whose name was Wentz, nodded. "The things them buggers won't think of! Save 'em for Williams; he'll sure want a look at them."

We rolled into Benson like a four-alarm fire and pulled up with a flourish before the stage office. The two passengers got out looking whey-faced and shaken. I tossed down their luggage while Wentz went in with the chest and mail sack to make his report. I tried not to think of that pair I'd shot.

Wentz came back, climbed to his seat and drove on around for fresh teams. He said, "We head on home soon's they back them fresh broncs into the harness. A three-hour run. Barrin' more trouble we'll be back before dark. Deputy's sendin' a couple men with a wagon to fetch in them cadavers."

An hour and a half later, with a full load of passengers, we reached the place where I'd dropped the two would-be stage robbers. One still lay at the side of the road, but the other was gone, which made me feel a mite less queasy. I'd never shot a man before in all my life and today I'd already killed two. Both, of course, had been trying to kill me, but they stuck like burrs at the back of my mind.

"You all right?" Wentz asked.

"Sure."

"Thought you looked a mite peaked. If it's them cadavers that's naggin' you, put 'em outa your mind. Better them than you is the way you gotta look at it. Them kind of buggers has got no more scruples than a starvin' bobcat."

I reckoned he was right, but I figured I'd had about enough of stagecoaching.

We came into Tombstone half an hour before dark, let the passengers off at the Wells-Fargo depot, tossed down their luggage, took in the mail sack and strongbox and drove on down to the West End Corral; left the coach and the horses and headed for a hash house to settle our stomachs. After which Wentz went one way and I picked up my mare and rode back to Fry's.

I wasn't hardly inside my room when somebody knocked. When I opened the door Josephina showed me her gamine's grin. "Where you been all day?"

"Jostlin' around on a Wells-Fargo stage playin' shotgun messenger. Been to Benson and back."

"No future there," she said, dismissing it. "Listen— I've got news. Nellie Cashman came by! She's offered to lease us the dining room at the American Hotel—how's that for luck?"

She was fairly bursting with excitement.

I hated to heave cold water on her notion, but somehow I couldn't drum up much interest; some of my mood was probably a carry-over from losing the money I'd put into the Russ House, but mostly, I guess, it was the result of discovering what I could do with a handgun.

She caught hold of my arm. "We can get Flick to help and be back in business."

"Guess you think quite a lot of Flick."

Her glance kind of sharpened. "Well, he *is* pretty handy you'll have to admit."

I was minded to name other things he was handy at but managed to stifle this dog-in-the-manger impulse. I finally said, "Have you looked at this place? How much work has to be done on it?"

"It's big enough. Been closed for a while but with a fresh coat of paint and a little redecorating we can take a lot of customers away from Pascholy and, to me anyway, that's worth thinking about."

I said indifferently, "How much is she asking for this run-down place?" Then I thought of something else. "Where's it located?"

"On Fremont near Fifth and we can have a year's lease for five hundred—"

"And next year, I reckon, it'll be a couple of thousand."

"You *are* in a hell-tearing mood. What's the matter with you, Alfie?"

"I sank close to fifteen hundred into that other place—"

"And you must have got most of it back the way we were packing them in. Look," she said in a wheedling fashion, "I'll put up the money and pay you a salary to manage the place. Oh, come on—say yes; you don't want to ride shotgun the rest of your life. Maybe it'll change your luck," she said, grinning. "Flick would go for it."

That did it! "But I'm paying half the freight on this deal. I'll take a salary to manage it and you'll take a bigger one for your talents as cook. Go ahead, sign us up."

Her face lit. She flung her arms round my neck, gave me a peck on the cheek. "You won't regret it," she assured me, excited as a kid who'd been promised a rare treat. Don't you want to come with me?"

I shook my head. "Have fun," I grumbled, reaching for my wallet.

"You can pay me later," she said, eyeing me, I thought, rather oddly. "Really, Alfie"—I didn't see any dimples, but she had her grin working—"I'm tickled to think we'll be partners in this."

Ten

NEXT MORNING, EARLY, I arrived at the depot packing the same load of gloom and mixed-up notions I'd taken to bed the night before. Perhaps it was not so much those shootings that had put me into this querulous mood as the many setbacks and frustrations I'd accumulated since getting off that train from New York, so bright of eye and eager to embrace the land of my dreams.

I'd lost in the interim a good many of the illusions I'd brought to this big-skyed western country and ought by now, I told myself, to look at things as they actually were and not as I'd hoped and imagined them to be. So why did I feel like a man on the brink? I'd thought long ago to have control of my temper, yet inside me now there was, I could feel, a seething mass of indescribable notions rushing me toward some final disaster.

It was this frame of mind, brushing past the clerk, that I took into the agent's office. Looking up from a pile of papers, Williams started to speak, stared more sharply and said, "What's got you into such a sweat?"

"I can't do it," I growled like a fool, "can't do it, I tell you!"

"Can't do what?"

"Work for this stageline! If I've got to kill people I've got to have a lot better reason than protecting the interests of Wells-Fargo and Company!"

74

He eyed me awhile without saying anything. Still staring, he bit the end off a cigar, opened a cash box that sat on his desk and tossed me a five dollar bill. Rasping a match on the desk's underside, he fired up to say through the smoke, "That will pay for your ride on the Benson stage. Shut the door as you leave."

"I've not gone yet." I put the two shotgun shells down in front of him, ignoring the bank note. "I watched you load that gun and just as I was about to climb up to the box; it was you who put the gun in my hands. Someone's been tampering with your stock of cartridges. Somebody working here is in cahoots with them bastards!" I said, and stomped out.

I got on my mare, hailed a passing citizen and asked where to find the sheriff.

Taking a squint at the sun, this fellow said, "Prob'ly be at the calaboose now."

Wheeling the mare, I rode east to Sixth, turned right for Toughnut and rounded the corner. As it happened Johnny Behan was just leaving the jail. I hailed him to ask for directions to Galeyville. He peered at me curiously.

"What're you wanting to go over there for?"

"Private business," I said to him, scowling.

"That's a long, rough ride. You'll want the east side of the Cherrycows, Turkey Creek Canyon—Curly Bill's old hangout. If you're bound to stick your nose in that hornet's nest you better take this along," he said, and handed me a deputy's badge. "I don't guarantee it'll keep you alive but it may give those buggers somethin' to think about."

He was right about the length of the ride, I discovered. Gave me a chance to sort of pull myself together. I had to make a dry camp to pass the night before venturing into those magnificent mountains. The grandeur of nature had been given full scope, an awesome vision of cliffs and rimrock, upthrust peaks and mighty gorges, a real devil's playground of nature in the raw.

Following Behan's directions, around eleven o'clock next morning I finally came into Galeyville where it perched on its mesa. Not much of a town compared to Tombstone, it housed perhaps some four hundred persons, mostly bad eggs by the look of the faces.

It had grown up in the wake of John Galey's discovery of silver in the fall of 1880 and the subsequent building of a smelter. And here it stood in a kind of amphitheater ringed by the mountains, the great bulk of the Cherrycows off to the west.

Its principle street flanked the edge of the mesa overlooking Turkey Creek. On the opposite side in solitary splendor was Nick Babcock's honky-tonk, a drink and dance emporium with some pretensions to elegance. It was said Curly Bill used to sit beneath the live oak in front of Nick's place banging away at everything that moved.

I was pleased he was not there to welcome me.

For no special reason except what I'd heard of Mollie McCarthy, I pulled up and dismounted at the hitch rack fronting Jack McCann's Last Chance Saloon. And there she was, Jack's pride and joy, his Thoroughbred mare, faster I'd been told than greased lightning. She certainly looked like a horse built to run. I gave her an approving nod of the head before pushing through the swing doors of the place.

McCann was back of the bar palavering with a man who had a foot on the rail and a mug in his mitt. With a shift of his glance he recognized me from a night he'd eaten in my Old Spain restaurant at the Russ House. "Addlington, shake the fist of my trainer. He's gettin' Mollie set for a race I've entered at the Watervale track.

"Tim," he said to the man with the beer, "this is the Last Chance Kid from Broken Butte. Runs the best eatin' house in Tombstone."

"Not anymore," I told them, and tapped the badge Behan had hung on me. "I'm looking for a man named Spence—Pete Spence. You got any notion where I might find him?"

I caught a brief blur of motion off to the right, a jingle of spur rowels and a rapid thud of departing boots. "There he goes now!" cried McCann, jerking a thumb toward the swinging batwings.

I lunged for them, swearing, and got out just in time to see that son of a bitch taking off on Mollie McCarthy. "Hellsafire!" Jack yelled in a fright as I was lifting my persuader, "don't throw down on him now—you'll hit that mare!"

This newest frustration nearly made me ignore him. I threw a wild look at the line of hitched horses. "Ain't nothin' around here can overtake Mollie," Jack's trainer opined.

Ignoring the lot of them, I swung aboard Singlefoot and took out after Spence. But it did not take a great while to convince me. After about five minutes with the gap increasing, I pulled my mare up and rode her back to the saloon. To have missed that little swindler by so narrow a margin was enough to cramp rats.

"Is there anyone round here can track that bastard?"

"Well," McCann said, "that old Apache we call Pop-Eye might do it—used to scout for General Crook when he was after Geronimo."

"Where do I find him?"

"I'll send one of the boys for him," Jack said. "I'd sure hate to have that mare stove up. Be a few minutes—come in an' wet your whistle."

Twenty minutes later the fellow came back with a tall, stringy Indian about the color of saddle leather, wearing a band of red cloth round his shoulder-length hair and not much else.

McCann introduced us. He said, "Pete Spence just rode off on my mare. Deputy here is goin' after her and wants you along to make sure he finds them."

"Me find 'em," said the old Indian with a gap-toothed grin.

"Let's get at it," I growled, and we set off at a lope, Pop-Eye in the lead and me right behind him.

Spence, after putting a few hills behind him, had dropped into a less hell-bent pace but was certainly up to all the dodges when it came to throwing pursuit off his tracks. Pop-Eye took all these subterfuges with a belittling grin. "Heap smart—me more smart," he chuckled, slogging right along. Instead of misleading us, Spence's bagful of tricks had done nothing but cut down his lead.

After some miles of steady riding, I began to have hopes of laying my hands on him. According to the Indian, the crook wasn't now more than ten minutes ahead of us. "Pretty soon see."

"Where's he heading for?"

"Mebbeso Portal—mebbe cut back toward Pearce."

We had come down out of the mountains now. The Apache said, "Mebbe San Simon," and pointed ahead. By straining my eyes, I presently made out a moving shape some miles ahead of us.

According to what I'd heard of the place, including women and kids, there were not above thirty people making their homes here. Place consisted of a saloon, a general store, some stock pens, several adobe huts and the newly laid tracks of the Southern Pacific. Plus a water tank that I could plainly see, setting off by itself.

Spence, though in sight, was still a good piece ahead of us, but unless he could grab a fresh horse in a hurry, he would have to fort up in one of the buildings.

Pop-Eye was riding a skinny paint pony with a great deal more endurance than I'd ever expected. A gelding it was, and the old man, seeing the approving look I'd bent on it, said, "Him papa racehorse—heap good pony."

But all my thinking was fixed on Pete Spence. The Indian had an old Sharps on his saddle. All I had was a six-shooter and the shotgun I had fetched from Lincoln.

Spence, it looked like, had no rifle. He'd not hold me off very long with a belt gun.

It was just about then I saw the smoke from a train.

. I kicked the mare into a hard, lurching run. Pop-Eye was lifting the Sharps when I yelled, "Don't shoot!" thinking he might hit McCann's mare.

He twisted his head to eye me, surprised. I said, "If you hit that mare McCann is like to kill both of us. Wait till he gets off her."

Eleven

WE WERE NOW moving up on Spence pretty fast as the work train's engine went chuffing past. But I could see we weren't moving fast enough. That five-car train of flats heavily loaded with rails and ties wasn't much more than just barely moving on this uphill grade.

Cursing now, I saw the fugitive, flanking the tracks, making ready to abandon McCann's lathered mare. And then he was off her, running alongside that laboring train. With a great leap and scramble he boarded the last car.

"Give me that Sharps!" I snarled at Pop-Eye, and snatching the rifle, I squeezed off a shot, cursing as Spence lunged out of sight behind a pile of ties. He must have realized then I had a one-shot rifle, for he popped up his head to thumb his nose at me. And that was the last I saw of him, as the train chugged off in the direction of Steins Pass.

I gave Pop-Eye back his rifle and a ten-dollar bill for services rendered, and a quarter hour later, with Mollie in tow, he set off on the long ride back to Galeyville.

Going over to the saloon, I procured a bar rag, wiped down my mare and walked her around for about half an hour, conscientiously cooling her out before belly-ing up the bar to try and settle my temper with a pair of tall beers.

The barkeep said, "Looked like Spence you boys was chasin'—what's he done now?"

I dropped some change on the bar and tromped outside, still too riled to trust my voice.

Getting back in the saddle, I rode leisurely over to Pearce, spent the night there and came into Tombstone about noon of the next day, leaving Singlefoot at the pole in front of the sheriff's office.

"You find him?" Behan asked.

"Found him and lost him," I said, and put up a hand to unpin his badge.

"Keep it," Behan said, "might come in handy. Heard you put in some time with Cap Mossman. Be glad to sign you on as a regular. That Wells-Fargo clerk says you're pretty sharp with that iron."

"I've about had my fill of killin'," I muttered.

"Well, keep it awhile anyhow," Behan urged. "Good men are hard to find around here. Should you change your mind your pay starts today." He eyed me awhile. "What happened to Spence?"

I told him. He said, "Be no loss if he never comes back, but I imagine he will. That kind of bad penny always turns up."

"Hope you're right," I growled, feeling mean.

Leaving him then, I rode up Sixth and west on Fremont till I reached the deep, narrow building that housed the American Hotel, owned jointly at this time by Nellie Cashman and a Mrs. Cunningham, who managed it. "My name's Addlington," I said, and she smiled. "I guess you're that Last Chance Kid Josephina has been telling me about. She has leased our restaurant, as you probably know. They've been doing it over. Why don't you go back? I'm sure they'll both be delighted to see you."

I stared at her blankly. "Right through there," she said, "at the end of the hall. Just follow the paint smell."

I was not at all sure I wanted Josephina for a partner. Though she was an exceptionally good cook and certainly didn't lack for confidence, she had, I thought, a rather bossy way, taking a great deal for granted, and an irritating way of wanting to manage things. Even when she was right, this could be pretty aggravating. Nor could I like the way Flick seemed to be always hanging around her.

He was with her now, both of them busily engaged in putting up the decorations we'd had at the Russ House.

Of a sudden, as though somehow sensing my presence, Josephina spun round in a swirl of skirts and a gamine's screech. "Alfie!" she cried, her whole face lighting up, and she came flying to fling both arms around me in so vigorous an embrace it pushed a grunt out of me. "I'm *so* glad you've come back! Aren't you, Flick? Just like old times!"

Across her shoulder I had a good view of Flick, who was certainly not revealing such unbridled enthusiasm. "The Last Chance Keed," he said with curled lip, and went off to hang up the red sombrero he was holding.

Josephina kissed me on both cheeks after the Mexican manner, then stepped back the better to appraise me. "Tell us what you've been doing and where you have been and—what's this? Are you a sheriff now?" she demanded, showing me her dimples.

"A kind of part-time deputy."

"You'll be too busy for that—you must geef it up. We've been counting on you to take charge of our venture . . . Isn't that so, Flick?"

"I guess so," Farsom said, still surveying the sombrero.

"Some of our old customers have come by to wish us luck. Do say you'll come in with us!"

"Have to give it some thought," I said, still watching Flick. "Have you quit your job with Dad Peppin, Farsom?"

"Yeah. Got no time for it."

"You see?" I said to her. "Being a deputy can be pretty exacting."

"Pooh!" she cried, wrinkling her nose. "If Flick's an example it's a lazy man's job. Don't you want to be my partner, Alfie?"

"I don't know."

She grew serious then and gave me a long, rather puzzled look. "You're not mad weeth me, are you?"

"No."

Still probing my face, she caught hold of my arm. "This will be no good unless you are part of it. I've such great plans—wait till you hear!"

"Well . . ." I temporized, "I might give it a try—for a month, say. See how it works out." If it had been just her and me . . . but with Flick hanging around I didn't know if I could stomach it. But I dug out my wallet and handed her five fifties, taking in his gone-still shape from the corners of my eyes, reckoning it was worth it to shove a spoke in his wheel. So pleased she was she went up on her toes in her extravagant manner to plant a firm kiss right smack on my mouth. Then, stepping back, she looked almost as startled as I was myself.

Next time I saw Johnny Behan I told him I'd become a partner in a restaurant business. "The Old Spain's opening in the American Hotel and—"

Grinning, he said, "Congratulations!" and punched my shoulder. "That girl's a real go-getter. Used to be a flamenco dancer up at Broken Butte, I'm told—really packed them in! But you can still be my deputy. I'll try not to take up too much of your time."

"Well . . . I been thinking. Any reason we can't put out a handbill on Spence? If I put up the money?"

"Been thinkin' about that myself, but couldn't figure where the money would come from. That hombre's about as hard to lay hold of as quicksilver. Every time I figure to have something on him he manages to wriggle clear." He looked down at the paper I pushed over his desk. "Fraud . . . yeah, and horse stealin'—that ought to do it. Take it over to Clum at the *Epitaph*. A rush job, tell him. Sheriff's office'll pay for it. Tell Clum we'll want five hundred copies."

The printer had the dodgers ready that evening.

REWARD

$500 will be paid for information leading to the arrest and conviction of PETE SPENCE, con man and tinhorn gambler, wanted for fraud and horse stealing.

Apply SHERIFF'S OFFICE, Tombstone.

' Reading it, Behan nodded. "Send about a hundred of these to the various sheriffs' offices, not forgettin' Nogales or Bisbee. I'll put a bunch of them around town, in Charleston and Pearce, Tucson, Mammoth and other roundabout places. We'll send the rest to the Post Office Department for additional distribution. Too bad you didn't include his description."

"Damn!" I said. "Guess I figured everybody knew him."

"We'll try it, anyway. Reckon he'll stay holed up for a while. Might even take off for greener pastures. Which would save you some money while gettin' him out from underfoot."

I was about to depart when he said, "Like for you to take a paseo over Charleston way. A note from one of the mill bosses—anonymous of course—says they think some of that road-agent bunch are hanging out over there. You might look into it."

I set out straightaway. Charleston was no great distance. When the wind was right we could hear the stamps crushing ore over there. I was content with the mare's easy rocking-chair gait, wood smoke and supper smell riding the air currents.

I sauntered into a hash house and put a solid meal inside me, afterward loitering in several saloons to listen to the gab with my badge out of sight. I didn't hear any mention of Spence, but there was plenty of comment and speculation about the current epidemic of stage stickups and the hurt being inflicted on mine owners to the increasing detriment of Wells-Fargo profits.

The average man in the street, as the saying goes, was not much concerned with the losses inflicted on the stage company, which was generally regarded as a greedy monopoly squeezing the little fellows into starvation and afterward buying them up for a song. This feeling, I gathered, was becoming so prevelant you could hardly get anyone to inform on the robbers, in consequence of which any number of persons down on their luck considered Wells-Fargo legitimate prey.

It was getting along toward midnight when, in one of the bars, I caught an unguarded word from a table nearby where three cowhands sat with their heads together over filled mugs of beer. Giving them a covert inspection, I finished my own and went out through the batwings.

Untying Singlefoot, I led her back into the deeper shadows of a closed mercantile establishment and took up a stance beside her. I didn't have to wait long before three rannies came out and got into their saddles.

Giving them a good start, I swung into leather and jogged along after them, staying far enough back to barely keep them in sight. This was no great chore, the night being what it was. I watched them disappear under the bridge.

The word I'd caught in the saloon was "stage," so I settled myself to do some more waiting. There was a great deal of that in a deputy's trade.

Some twenty minutes later I caught the sound of fast-moving horses and the rattle and bang of a coach approaching, and watched the trio, faces hidden behind pulled-up wipes, come out of the shadows and climb onto the bridge armed with rifles.

Leaving the mare on grounded reins, I slipped under the bridge to where they'd left their horses. I heard the crack of a Winchester, a shout and the mutter of voices as the stage shrieked to a stop. "Throw down that box an' be quick about it!"

I heard the box hit the road and was tempted to go up there, then a better notion came to me, and when the coach moved off with consequent racket, I looped the reins of the robbers' horses round the horns of their saddles and sent them pelting off along the shore toward town.

Very soon I head the slither of boots as the robbers with their loot came lurching into the deeper dark that was concealing me from them.

"Hey! Where the hell's them horses?" somebody growled, and the three of them stopped, their shapes showing plainly against the lesser dark behind.

"Just shuck them shooters, boys, and haul your hands up over your bonnets."

But one of those fools made a grab for his iron. He let out a wild yell as my shot swept his hand away from it. "And don't let go of that box," I told the others. "Now pick up those rifles."

It was easy as that.

With two of them lugging the Wells-Fargo chest and that third galoot lugging the Winchesters, I marched them up to where I'd left Singlefoot and, swinging into the saddle, herded them along to the Charleston calaboose. Stopping them alongside the the hitching rack, I shouted, "Wake up in there! I've got some boarders for you!"

Out came two deputies, both with drawn pistols.

"Three stage robbers with loot. Get 'em locked up. I'll be round in the morning and take them off to Tombstone."

Twelve

BRIGHT AND EARLY next morning I came by with buck-board and driver, saw the Wells-Fargo chest stored behind the seat and relieved the Charleston jail of my manacled prisoners. There was a bandage around the wounded man's arm. I climbed into my saddle and followed them to Tombstone.

Behan, coming out, stood looking them over. "Nice work," he grunted. "That feller with the wrappin' we been hunting for months."

We fetched them inside. "Whatever's in your pockets just leave there on the desk," said Behan after searching them for weapons. I took off their bracelets and we locked them into separate cells. "We'll have 'em up for a preliminary hearin' sometime this afternoon," the sheriff said after we returned to his office. "I'm going to have to get over to Tucson tonight—be gone a few days probably. While I'm away you'll be in charge."

Judge heard the case that afternoon and bound them over. Behan had thought some of changing the venue but eventually decided to try them right here. Next morning he boarded the stage for Tucson. Only reason I could figure he hadn't left last night was that he likely slept better in his own accustomed bed.

• • •

While I'd been away the new Old Spain restaurant had opened for business, so along toward the shank of the afternoon I took Singlefoot over to the American Hotel and went in to sample some of Josephina's cooking.

She had an attractive Mexican girl waiting on tables, and Farsom was on a stool back of the cash register. When I gave him a nod, he looked at me sourly. I wondered what had put his nose out of joint. He'd changed considerable since we'd quit the Russ House. Whenever I came round it seemed like my presence annoyed him.

Ignoring his surliness, I pulled out a chair at a corner table where his glowering wouldn't spoil my meal and gave the girl my order.

Though it was a bit early for supper the place was already about half-filled with diners, many of them well-dressed persons of substance. Looked a pretty safe bet Josephina was going to make a real go of this. Several of our old Russ House clientele smiled at me or nodded. Probably surprised to see me packing a badge. I noticed one of the Earps was eating here this evening. He chucked me a solemn-faced nod.

Josephina herself came along with my meal and her gamine grin said how pleased she was. "I've got to get back to the kitchen," she murmured. "I have a pretty good helper and a girl to wash dishes but right now, anyway, I have to oversee everything. What do you think of hiring someone with a guitar to play for the dinner crowd?"

"Sounds all right to me. What's ailin' Flick? Every time I show up he acts like a scorpion has crawled up his pant leg."

"I expect he's jealous. Wants me to marry him and . . ."—she looked at me quizzically—"seems to think you're the reason I keep telling him no."

Reckon I looked astonished. "Must have bats in his belfry."

"Ho!" she said with flashing eyes. "You theenk he's loco? *Cuidado, hombre!* He's not the only one who weesh to marry me!"

"Bully for you," I said with a grin. "You're a fine-looking female—don't blame 'em a bit."

Flinging back her mop of black hair with a furious look, she went stalking off in her tigerish stride. "Smart, too," I called after her, ignoring the stares. I did notice Earp's eye regarding me with an open speculation and cursed the heat flushing up from my collar.

The food had been fixed with exceptional care and settled into my stomach like a lump of lead. I can't think what ailed me, but I was in a sod-pawing mood when I threw down my napkin and jounced out of my chair with that delectable supper no more than half-eaten. I did have sufficient regard for my position in the community, however, to fire up a stogie and, with this jutting from my face at a jaunty angle, headed for the door.

As I strode past the cash register, Flick, on his stool, muttered, "If you can't show her a little respect—"

I spun round on a heel to fix hot eyes on him. "How much *dinero* have you put into this place?"

He shrunk away from my look with a darkening face. Naked hate was in the glare he turned on me as I shoved past to stamp down the hall in a fiercening temper.

Piling into the saddle and still seething, I pulled up in front of the Tombstone calaboose. Inside I dropped smoldering into Behan's swivel back of the desk, staring into my future, minded right then to have done with that restaurant and everything in it, remembering my hunch she'd be trouble the first time I'd seen her. So caught up had I got in this briar patch of notions I scarcely noticed the bug-eyed looks being loosed by the deputies on tap.

When I noticed, I growled "What the bloody hell are you starin' at?" and both of them made haste to find other things to engage their attention. Digging out my wallet, I saw there was not enough in it to take care of the reward I'd slapped on Pete Spence, and I'd not yet heard anything from the post office at Lincoln, to which three weeks past I'd sent a request to have my mail forwarded. I thought if it wasn't one damn thing it was half a dozen others.

I got up and took myself back into the cell block to have a look at my prisoners, and there were no prisoners there.

I thought my eyes were surely playing tricks, but if tricks had been played, my eyes had no part in them. I went with clenched jaws back into the office.

"How long you fellows been here?"

The big-shouldered older one, Dry Camp Hazelton, allowed they'd been holding down the benches all afternoon. "Except," he said, "for the ten minutes or so it took me to go by for the mail." With a level-eyed look, he said, "It's all right there in front of you on the desk."

"What about you, Fanshaw?"

"Been right here," the cocky younger man grunted.

I didn't care for the way his look eluded mine. "The whole afternoon?"

"That's right."

"What time did you feed the prisoners?"

Dry Camp said, "Ain't fed 'em yet—come to that we ain't et either."

I told him, "Go take a look at them."

Dry Camp got up, and a couple moments later he shouted, "What the hell is this?" and came back on the run.

"Where are your horses?" I asked Fanshaw.

"Tied to the hitch rail."

"Go fetch one of them in here."

He looked like he figured I had lost all my marbles, but got up off his butt. "My mare," I said, "is the only horse out there."

Dry Camp, looking startled, said, "You sayin' somebody's stole 'em?"

"How come you never noticed when you came back with the mail?"

"Reckon my mind must've been on somethin' else."

"By God," I said, looking hard at Fanshaw, "you better find them prisoners and get them back here pronto!"

Sullenly he muttered, "Don't take it out on me—*I* never lost them. You're the one Behan left in charge!"

Something seen in my face must have punctured his belligerence. He went off through the door like a scuttling rabbit.

Dry Camp growled, "You reckon he turned them fellers loose?"

"One of you did."

"Yeah," he said. "Well, it sure wasn't me."

Thirteen

SEEMED A PRETTY futile hope to harbor any expectation of recovering them now, for they'd be putting every mile possible between themselves and this calaboose. It occurred to me presently what we were dealing with here was three escaped robbers with only two horses, unless they'd managed to pick up another mount. Bound to try to, that was certain. One horse for two rannies would slow their departure considerable.

In that hodgepodge of tracks outside there was no way you could sort out what sign they had left. If I'd had that old Apache here . . .

"Dry Camp," I said, "anyone round here that's good at reading sign?"

"Wyatt Earp's pretty good. Sheriff is, too—"

"Go see if Wyatt's in a mood to go hunting."

He was back with Earp inside of ten minutes. Dry Camp, I guessed, had explained the problem. Earp was busily studying the ground. He squatted down for a closer look, presently got up and said, shaking his head, "Can't hardly tell one set from the others. Too many going every whichway."

Then he wrinkled up his face and tugged at his mustache. "Be a far-out chance, but one of them rannies used to ride with Curly Bill. I'd say Galeyville would be your best bet."

Thanking him, I sent Dry Camp off to get himself a horse, and twenty minutes later we set out for the Cherrycows. "Expect you know this country better than me. We'll waste no time hunting tracks. I'm leaving it to you to pick the shortest route."

"That damn fool Fanshaw," he grumbled after a spell of silent riding. "Why d'you reckon he turned them fellers loose?"

When I shrugged he said, "You reckon one was a particular friend?"

"I expect he was bribed—scairt, maybe."

"Hell, you seen what they had in their pockets. Not enough between 'em to choke a baby gopher!"

"Yeah. Likely threatened him." I swore disgustedly. "This will probably turn out to be a wild goose chase."

"Like enough," Dry Camp agreed. "Couple years back the Earps an' that Wells-Fargo feller, Fred Hume, chased a bunch of stage robbers more than six hundred miles an' all they got out of it was the feller that held their horses." He peered at me. "What you figure to tell Behan when he gits back?"

"Tell him they broke out, I guess."

"He ain't goin' to like it."

"Don't like it myself. I suppose I ought to have locked up Fanshaw. I could wring his worthless neck. Might do it yet if we don't come up with them." I could see plain enough their loss was my responsibility.

Out on these flats it was getting hotter than hell's backlog. I was mopping my face when Dry Camp said, "It'll be plumb dark inside half an hour. You reckon we oughta make camp?"

"We're pushin' right on."

Dry Camp said, "That's a right nice mare you're forkin'. Comfortable gait an' plenty of bottom. Be glad to have one like her myself."

We came in due course to a kind of wild-looking trough heavily filled with night's shadows between nearly straight-up walls. "Silver Creek Canyon," Dry Camp commented. "Be pretty rough goin' for a while with all this brush an' rock. Things'll be goin' full tilt time we git up there on that mesa."

When we got into its canyon I recognized Turkey Creek from the other time I was up here after Pete Spence. I reckoned we were inching up on our goal, and high time, too. Must have been not too short of midnight.

Dry Camp said, "Mill's shut down. In the old days you could of heard it plain ridin' where we are now. You wanta watch your step up there—lotta Curly Bill's crowd still hangin' around an' they ain't real partial to deppities. You'd never catch Behan ridin' up here."

Through saddle screak and jingling spur chains we could hear the distant shouts and fiddle squeal. Babcock's place, I thought to myself. And Dry camp grunted, "Pretty nigh there," and jerked his head toward the distant lights that were like the luminescence of glow worms high above us. "Don't hardly seem natural without Curly's six-shooter bangin' away."

I could certainly do without that.

Should we come onto our quarry, I had little doubt but what fireworks would follow. You couldn't picture those three riding all this way only to give up without a shot.

"Where," I said, "do you expect we'll find them?"

"Babcock's deadfall, if they're still around," he said, and added disparagingly, "Keeps three, four females on tap to help the customers get rid of their money."

We were riding now, walking our horses through an even darker swirl of confusing shadows beneath a black tangle of remembered ash and sycamore, and coming presently out of these, we found the trail lurching upward in its climb to the mesa.

And there ahead of us, in the rumble of racket from the long row of saloons on the left hand and Babcock's in lone-wolf fashion on the other, was another of the camps that had mushroomed on silver. Gambling and drinking was a night-and-day industry.

In the light spilling out of these various enterprises you could see the huddles of horses waiting at the racks for their inebriated masters. At Babcock's both rails were packed solid. As we dismounted off to one side, Dry Camp, nudging me, pointed. "There's my Sugarfoot hoss," he muttered. "Reckon them three is here all right."

"Might's well get at it," I said, and shoved through the swinging doors, Dry Camp right at my heels.

The long room was ablaze with Rochester lamps swung from the beams of the smoke-darkened roof. The piano man was having himself a beer break, but the foot-tapping fiddler was sawing his way through "The Camptown Races" while three couples whirled about the small hunk of floor not given over to gambling layouts.

The three stage robbers were in the line of men bellying up to the bar, and for perhaps two, three minutes we appeared to be unnoticed. Then the fiddler quit fiddling, and in the comparative quiet one of the escaped prisoners twisted his head and spotted us. Before he could open up a yell, the speaking end of a pistol was shoved into my back. "Easy, boy," Dry Camp said, free hand snaking the iron off my hip. "Easy does it." He stepped back with a chuckle. "Easy as guttin' a slut," he declared, vastly pleased with himself.

I was mad enough to put a fist in his face but thought better of it and stood bitterly glaring at having once more been played for a sucker. The three escapees, with a couple of their half-drunk cronies, all joined hands and went capering about me, grinning like fools as they jumped and skipped and hopped and shouted, looking as if they had just got loose from some mental institution. And the honky-tonk piano man tinkled big fingers up and down the keys while another damn nitwit joined in with a jug.

When the hand clapping quit and the dancers stood panting, Dry Camp asked, "What we gonna do with him?"

"Hang the son of a bitch!" somebody yelled.

And another one shouted, "Tar an' feathers!"

"Drop him down a well!"

"Seriously," Dry Camp urged when a lull gave him a chance to be heard, "Alfie here could be a fine hole card if we manage it right," and some tall galoot yelled, "Run him through the stamps!"

Just about then I caught a glimpse of Jack McCann elbowing his way to the front. "Boys," he called, "this here's the varmint that chased my mare clean over to San Simon. A plumb awful thing he done to ol' Mollie an' me havin' to scratch her out of that race. Feels like I orta have some say in what's to be done with him."

"All right, Jack. You got the floor."

"I wanta think up somethin' that'll be real fittin'. How about lockin' him into that empty ice house till I kin dredge up somethin' real fittin'?"

After more arguing and horsing around that's where they put me with the whole push jostling along to be sure I got put in there with no way to get loose.

Fourteen

IF YOU'VE EVER been into a country ice house, you'll have some idea of what the place smelled like. It was larger than most, built to take care of the whole town through the summers when the mill was running, but all that was in it right now besides me was a lot of stinking sawdust. Though it was intended to be airtight, the heat of the hot months had opened some seams. I was able to breathe, but in that black hole with nothing for company but bitter thoughts, it was a long night indeed.

Just prior to cock crow I heard the crunch of boots. McCann with his face pressed to one of the cracks said, "I've fetched ye some vittles an' a flask of sour mash. I'll open this door far enough fer you to reach 'em. But you try any stunts an' I'll blow your fool head off— savvy?"

He eased the door open about six inches with a foot braced against it, free hand gripping the butt of a pistol. I grabbed the pistol and he slammed the door shut. "You ungrateful bastard! Go ahead an' starve!" he said, and I heard the crunch of his boots moving off. It was a sure bet he'd gone off with the food and flask. Having them found would have caused a commotion.

At least now I had a gun, utterly useless against that barred door. I could find little hope in my situation.

When they came after me I might shoot two or three. Make them mad enough to put a slug through my head. I wasn't going under those stamps if I could help it.

And then I heard boots approaching once more, and the accompanying mutter of bickering voices. From the snatches of talk I was able to decipher I guessed it was the stage robbers out there now. Dry Camp apparently had gone back to town.

"But why'd he want to bring that limey out here?"

"To git rid of him, of course. Figgered to let us do the killin'," someone else said, cursing. "Put his nose outa joint when Behan put this foreigner over him. He kin tell any yarn he wants to now, blame Fanshaw for us gittin' loose. Who's t' say he's lyin'?"

"Let's get this door open an' shoot the little bugger."

"I dunno," one of the others said. "Why not let McCann take care of him? It was McCann's hoss he ruint."

"Jack's too soft—don't go fer this killin' stuff."

"Come to that I don't either. Let's leave him in there. He'll not last long with no food an' water.

The language I used was pretty Tabasco when they went off without opening the door. I understood Dry Camp a mite better now, and I'd offer odds Fanshaw by now had dug for the tullies. But these notions, like McCann's pistol, were of damn little use toward my getting out. And the air in this place was getting worse by the minute.

I was beginning to feel kind of light in the head when, with no sound at all to herald an approach, the bar was lifted and the door eased open. It was not yet quite day, and I could hear that damn piano and fiddle wail from Babcock's and some female's shrill laugh; but it was light enough now to discern bare feet and the skirted shape in the gap left by that opened door. A girl spoke in an urgent whisper. "Alfie! Can you hear me, Alfie?"

By God! *Josephina!* I was near undone by the relief galloping through me. I pulled fresh air deep into starved lungs. "How'd you get here? How'd—"

"Later," she said. "Come on—I've got a mount for you."

Onto my feet I glimpsed the gleam of a shotgun's barrel, but the desperate picture of what we were up against held me rooted in my tracks. "Have you got—?"

"Come *on*! They're down in the bottoms hitched to a sycamore."

I stared at her, astonished. "You mean you've got those three robbers . . ."

"No—of course not. But if you don't get a move on—"

"But what've you got tied up in the bottoms?"

"Horses!" she said, catching hold of me, pulling. "Don't you want—?"

"I'm not going back empty-handed," I growled, and she thrust the sawed-off into my hands. "Thanks. You go wait with the horses. I'll just be a minute."

I could feel her horrified stare. "Are you crazy?"

"I came after those road agents; I ain't leaving without 'em."

"*Estúpido!*" she cried, stamping her foot. "Go on, then—get yourself killed! I wash my hands of you!"

"Go wait with the horses," I growled, twisting away from her, but she flung me around with a strength born of terror. "You can't *do* this!"

"That place will be half-empty by now. Look for yourself; the only mounts in front of Nick's now are the ones they came on. Go fetch our horses and wait outside. Go on!"

I threw off her clutch and took my craziness straight for Babcock's, never looking back.

Fifteen

SHE WAS RIGHT! You could not call what I proposed reasonable, but there was a stubborn streak in me that refused to abandon a task once started. Bright in my mind were Evans's words to me at Lincoln; I was determined to put that authority to the test.

Halfway to Nick's deadfall a racket of pistol shots tore up the quiet from the far end of town. Ignoring this, not even throwing a look in that direction, I came up to the hitch rails in the deeper gloom underneath the live oak and paused by a window to see what I'd be up against. All those Rochester lamps were still lit.

Aside from the barkeep and one of the girls, the only persons in sight were the three I was after. I shoved through the louvered doors and was spotted at once by the skinniest robber, who goggled an instant before yelling at the others. A second robber whirled, reaching hipward while the third dumped the girl off his lap and tried frantic to get his feet under him. But the sight of that leveled Greener took a heap of the starch out of their intentions.

"Grab hold of your ears!" I flung at the apron, who made haste to obey. To the washed-out blonde I growled, "Get their guns and don't get in front of 'em . . . That's the ticket. Now throw them across the room and get down on the floor—belly down. You too!" I snarled at the barkeep. "If you've got a shooter you better stay clear of it. Once we've got out of here stay right where you are or I'll not be responsible for casualties."

He nodded, and I glanced through the window nearest the street. In the brightening light I could see Josephina sitting her saddle, reins of the spare mount trailing from one hand, a pistol clutched in the other. "All right, you three—out of here! Step lively now or I'll empty some hats."

With obvious reluctance, nervously eyeing my sawed-off, they moved through the batwings, me right on their heels. While the girl covered them with her pistol, I got aboard the spare horse. "Keep your horse at a walk and head for the bottoms ... All right, boys. Don't chance your luck."

I followed them down through the ash and sycamores and into the trail for Silver Creek, hearing no commotion behind us—not that I put any trust in this. Wanting mightily to step up the pace, I resisted the impulse, and still at a walk we followed Silver Creek out of the mountains. No one tried any tricks or opened his mouth. I guessed Evans was right about the authority of a shotgun.

Time we got out on the sunshiny flats I'd made up my mind there would be no pursuit. I told Josephina, "If it wasn't for you I'd still be in that ice house or hunting a harp and a halo. How'd you know where I was?"

"Asked around. Wyatt Earp said you were headed for Galeyville." She regarded me soberly. "What do we do now?"

"Put these fellows back where I had them," I said, not mentioning the score I aimed to settle with Dry Camp.

With one of those uncanny transferences of thought she said, "Ever since Behan took over as sheriff Dry

Camp has been his chief deputy; when Johnny put you over him I suspected there'd be trouble. I tried to steer you away from that job."

"I remember," I said. "I'd like to get Flick—"

"Flick's gone."

I threw her a sharp look. "What do you mean Flick's gone?"

"After you left Flick picked up his hat with a face like stone and walked out of there. I haven't seen him since."

I thought about this and several other things, including this girl who looked so fragile with her slim dancer's body and her quicksilver ways, mercurial, steadfast and wholly an enigma. What did she secretly think of us? More especially me—the Fool of Chance.

"You took a fearful risk coming after me like that . . ."

"Ho!" she scoffed. "I'm no stranger to Galeyville. I'm not afraid of those outlaws. I sang at Jack McCann's for a while when Curly Bill was still around."

We jogged along with no more talk for the next eight miles. Nearing Tombstone, riding through Charleston in the shade of those great cottonwoods along the west bank of the San Pedro, I gave some thought to Dry Camp and what he might do when he saw us dismounting in front of the calaboose. Probably grab for his iron and, after I was blasted, claim I was the one who had turned them loose. But with Fanshaw gone, if I should kill Dry Camp, who was left to back up my story? Josephina would probably, but she only knew part of it, the part she'd been concerned with.

We pulled up in front of the Tombstone jail, and no one came out to welcome our return. There were no horses at the tie rail, no passing vehicles, no pedestrians or horsebackers in this late afternoon quiet. Where was the sheriff? More to the point, where was Dry Camp? Making his rounds or lurking inside to pistol me from cover?

"Get down," I said to our three sullen prisoners, shotgun leveled.

The toughest of the three threw a searching look for possible help, let go his breath with a disgusted snort and dismounted, the other two following suit.

I handed Josephina the key to the gun rack and saw those bastards swapping covert looks. "Never mind," I grinned, handing her the sawed-off. "Just hold 'em steady till I get set . . . All right," I said from the doorway, persuader in hand. "Step right in."

I expect it was that shotgun in the hands of a girl that weighed heaviest with them. One by one they trooped inside with considerable chagrin but no arguments. I marshaled them into their former cells and slammed the gratings with a sigh of relief.

Having blown out that gusty breath I grinned. "Make yourselves right at home," I advised, and went back to the office, where I found Josephina slumped in Behan's swivel.

"I'm sure glad that's done," I said, and picked up the sawed-off she had left on the desk.

"Yes," she said, eyes searching my face. "What about Dry Camp?"

"Cross that bridge when I come to it." I dropped the ring of cell keys into my pocket. "Close the restaurant and try to get some rest—we'll eat out tonight."

She brightened at that and rose to put a hand on my arm. "Be careful, Alfie—please . . ."

After she'd gone I did considerable thinking, quite aware I wasn't done with this yet. Dry Camp had to be reckoned with, maybe Fanshaw too if he hadn't taken off. And there was Singlefoot, still like enough in Galeyville. I sure didn't want to lose her, having had her with me ever since Lincoln.

I rode over to the town marshal's office and found Virgil Earp with his boots on the desk. I said, "Seen anything of Fanshaw lately?"

"Nope. Last I seen he was on a horse travelin' south. Expect you've lost him."

"No loss. How about Dry Camp?"

"He's around someplace."

Thanking him, I rode up the street to the Wells-Fargo office. "Williams in?" I asked the clerk.

"Down the hall, second door to the right."

The agent sat back of his paper-cluttered desk. He put down his pencil and eyed me inquiringly. I said, "Got those three stage hold-ups locked in the jail and the keys in my pocket."

"You have?" He sounded surprised. "Never expected to see them again."

"Thought you might want Fred Hume over here to sit in with the prosecutor when they come up for trial."

"Yes," he said. "I'll be in touch with him." I read speculation back of his stare. "Been wonderin' about you since Dry Camp showed up riding solo. Flock of rumors jouncing around. Heard you'd been killed. Seems the prisoners, after he'd been knocked out, took out for the border. Another yarn has it you were in cahoots with 'em."

"Yes, well, you know how it is with rumors—ten cents a dozen."

"Mind tellin' me the straight of it?"

"I made quite a mess of it, not to dress the thing up in clean linen. Misplaced trust has been the story of my life." I told him what had happened, how Josephina got me out of the ice house and held the horses while I went after them. "Sure had me boiling when Dry Camp stuck that gun in my back."

"That all you got to say on the subject?"

"Reckon that's it."

"What do you figure to do about Dry Camp?"

"Arrest him, I reckon."

"Might take a bit of doing. That feller's no slouch with a pistol."

"Guess we'll just have to see."

I left him then and got back in the saddle. The shadows bent long and dark across Allen Street. Before much longer it would be plumb dark. Quickest way to locate Dry Camp was by drawing his fire, and I felt the risk as I toured the town. Passing through an alley, I came into Toughnut, still watchful, still looking, still probing the deeper shadows. I rode up one side and down the other, aware of the thrill seekers cautiously following.

Passing the Russ House, I turned up Fifth. Tried the Oriental without finding him.

Moving across Fourth, I continued west, passing through bars of lamplight spilling into the street, feeling the pressure, expecting any moment to get blown from the saddle.

I took to the middle of the street, back on Allen again, still looking. Breasting the schoolhouse I caught a shifting in the shadows by Dunbar's stable, the glint of a lifting gun barrel. I'd left the shotgun in Behan's office; I palmed my pistol.

Two shots rang out, very nearly together. I saw the swirl in the shadows, heard the thump as the top half of him banged into a wall.

Sliding off the horse, I ran forward, gun lifted, but all the fight was knocked out of him. In the flare of my match I heard him groan as I bent over him. There was blood on one pant leg, glistening in the match flame, My shot had caught him just below the thigh. I called, "Somebody get Doc McKee! He'll be needed at the sheriff's office. Couple of you boys get a blind off that house and take him over there."

I got back on the horse Josephina had fetched me at Galeyville and rode back to the calaboose. Leaving the horse on dropped reins, I went into Behan's office, took a squint at my prisoners, still snug and scowling, and went back and sat down behind Behan's desk to get the shake out of my legs while I waited for them to fetch Dry Camp.

It was there Williams found me.

Sixteen

THE VOICE OF the Wells-Fargo agent roused me out of my thinking. "I assume since you're not layin' out on the street congratulations are in order. What happened to Dry Camp?"

"He'll be along; couple of fellows will be fetching him directly. Took a bullet in the thigh."

"Too bad you didn't make a better job of it. Save the county some cash."

Two men filed in with Dry Camp groaning on the blind. "Where you want him?"

"Last cell opposite those stage robbers."

A buggy drove up and the doctor came bustling in with his bag. I took him back to the cells, thanked the pair who'd been transport for Dry Camp and asked them to replace the blind where they'd got it from. They went off with it.

Williams said, when I came back to the office, "Where'd you find him?"

"Stashed in the shadows by Dunbar's barn."

He shook his head. "I'll get off a wire to Hume tonight. Looks like your luck has taken a turn for the better."

Doc McKee came back from the cells with his bag. "He'll be able to get around in a week or so. Slug

109

missed the bone. I've given him a few drops of lau-
danum—probably sleep till noon. I'll come by in the
morning."

And off he went.

I washed up and put on a fresh shirt, reminded of my
date with Josephina. Leaving my horse at the Palace
Livery Stable, I hired a yellow-wheeled buggy and drove
to the American Hotel. Josephina, also spruced up, was
waiting in the lobby. Pleased me the way her face lighted
up when I came through the door. "That your buggy?"
she asked, surprised.

"Ours," I said. "Just rented for the occasion." Handing
her up, I asked, "Where shall we go?"

"How about the Can Can? Quong Key's a very good
cook, and you needn't eat Chinese food if you don't like
it." She smiled, bringing out her dimples. "He serves
gringo grub, too, you know."

"Whatever you want will suit me fine," I assured her,
and saw a sparkle come into the eyes searching mine.
"Nobody can beat you at cooking, Josie."

"And aside from that how do I strike you?"

"Well . . ." I said, considering the breath-held look
of her, "you needn't take a backseat in the shape department, and you're powerfully efficient . . ."

She made a face at me and settled resignedly onto the
cushion with a look that made a chuckle come out of me.
"Actually," I told her, throwing caution to the winds, "I
like everything about you."

"You do?" she said, astonished. A delighted smile
then reshaped her red lips. "You must have taken great
pains to keep me from knowing."

"Yeah—I'm the world's greatest chump."

"I don't care," she cried. With both arms around me,
she put her mouth against mine with great gusto. "Tell

me again," she urged through our panting.

I said, "We'll never get there if we keep this up." But we did, eventually. It was a night to remember. She snuggled against me all the way back to the American Hotel.

Next morning, when I arrived at the jail with the handful of mail I'd picked up, I went first of all to have a look at my stage robbers. They were still under duress, scowling and sullen. Dry Camp was asleep.

Back at Behan's desk I glanced through the mail. Mostly circulars, I judged from the envelopes. There was one tan-colored one addressed to me, very official looking, postmarked Lincoln. *At last!* I thought, and tore it open. Seemed a new man was postmaster there.

When I came on this job there were four letters for you which, with no idea of your whereabouts, I returned to sender, a firm of solicitors at Gray's Inn, London.

I read this three times before I got up enough wind to say what I thought of him.

For a long while I sat there absorbing this jolt. Then, remembering Josephina, I muttered, "To hell with it," and, crumpling the message, pitched it into the wastebasket just as Johnny Behan came into the office, stare rummaging my face. "What's botherin' you—more troubles?"

I pulled myself together. "You'll be needing a couple new deputies now that Fanshaw has skedaddled and Dry Camp's laid up from leaning against a bullet," I said, and right on cue, Doc McKee drove up and came tramping into the office, jerking us a nod as he went bustling off to the cell block with his little black bag.

"What's he doing here?" Behan asked, staring after him before hauling his attention back to me. "What was that about Dry Camp? Who shot him?"

"I did," I said, and gave him the gist of it. He stared at me like he couldn't believe it. "I'd have sworn by that feller. Not overly bright but . . . Shoved a gun in your back did he? Tried to dry-gulch you . . ." He grabbed hold of my hand with a grip that made my fingers ache. "By God, you done fine, Alfred—just fine!"

Shortly before my arrival in this hell-bending place, a small hospital had been built and staffed, so there was no real need to keep Dry Camp on tap, but the sheriff decided to do it anyhow. "I don't want him headin' for Texas before we get him tried and convicted! I'm going to throw the book at him—"

"Malfeasance in office is about all we've got on him, turning those road agents loose, and we'll have our work cut out proving that now Fanshaw's disappeared," I reminded him.

"Pullin' a gun on you and leaving you for them Galeyville ruffians to massacre and then, here in town, trying to dry-gulch you—"

"No evidence," I said. "You'll never get those Galeyville owlhooters to testify. I doubt," I said, "we can even prove malfeasance. Maybe we better forget the whole thing and save the taxpayers some money."

Johnny Behan scowled. "He's a treacherous dog. I'll think of something."

"I doubt we'll ever see Fanshaw again."

"We can put out a bulletin! The man's a material witness!"

"Better concentrate your energy on replacing them.

Ain't going to be easy—too much risk getting shot on this job."

Ten days passed before we got our first recruit, a young fellow by the name of Frisco Jones who certainly didn't appear to be more than fifteen but swore he was twenty. No kith nor kin if you could believe him. "I been a orphant far back's I can recollect," he told us earnestly. "You'll find I'm honest and have enough guts to cut the mustard, I reckon."

He was dressed like a cowhand, the floppy front brim of his hat pinned up with a cactus thorn, a real eager beaver. I was favorably impressed. Behan with reservations said he'd take him on trial, and the kid was sworn in. "Just sort of prowl around town," the sheriff told him, "and get to know it. And don't put a hand near that shooter without your figurin' to use it." He pinned a badge on Jones and turned him loose.

Second man we took on was a different breed of cat, bigger even than Dry Camp, with a look of hard usage and a Texas drawl, brown as boot leather and packing a pair of hooded eyes that were green as grass. Called himself Butterfly Smith.

"Don't remember ever seeing you around," Behan said, inquiring-like.

"Stands to reason. Come from clean back where the hoot owls roost, off beyond Peña Blanca. I been around an' kin hold my drinks with the best of 'em."

Behan, looking dubious, hired him. "You'll be on probation till I say different. We got a man back in the cells with a leg wound—go take a good look at him. Used to be my chief deputy. I don't want him getting sprung."

After Smith had gone off to have a look at Dry Camp, I said, "Reckon that Galeyville bunch will try to liberate him?"

"Might," Behan grumbled. "What do you think of this feller?"

"Hard as nails."

"My thought exactly. Got the look of a gunslinger. In a place like this that could be an asset. Case you ain't noticed, this office ain't none too popular round these here environs. Just as well to have an ace in the hole."

Just about then our buggy doc, McKee, put in an appearance to see how his patient was coming along. Coming back from the cells, he said, "Without he suffers a relapse this'll be my last call." He gave Behan his bill for services rendered, and the sheriff chucked it into a drawer with some others the county hadn't got around to paying.

As McKee left we got another visitor, who came in looking about as keyed up as a thundercloud. "Got a job for you, Behan." He was introduced to me as Mr. Farney, owner of the Tombstone Mining & Milling Company.

"What kind of job?" Behan asked.

"Payroll's missing—so's the feller who was keepin' my books," Farney said.

"Name and description."

"Thaddeus Manley. About five eight. Towhead with a diamond stickpin. Blue serge suit, high button shoes— wears galluses red as a fire engine. Talks like a banker and wears a bowler."

"We'll look into it," Behan promised. "How much did he take you for?"

"Around fifty-four hundred, near as I can figure," Farney said.

"You putting up a reward? Sometimes it helps."

"I ain't minded to throw good money after bad. Your

stipend comes outa the taxpayers. I'm a taxpayer. Get busy."

After he'd gone, Behan said, "Tough customer. Likes to give himself airs. You want to look into this, Alfred?"

"Sure," I said. "Reckon that embezzler will head for the border?"

"Your guess is good as mine."

I went outside and got on my horse. If this galoot was making for Mexico, the chance of coming up with him looked almighty slim. Tombstone boasted several hotels in addition to a flock of rooming houses like Fly's. Fellow might decide to hole up until the heat was off, so I started making the rounds. The lodging places first.

By the time I'd tried Addie Bourland's, the San Jose House—"Heat. Rooms with or Without"—Smith's, the San Francisco Lodging House, the warren of rooms above the Elite Café, Dutch Annie's, the place that had once been the Commercial Hotel and several of the less likely, my stomach said it was time to get fed, so I rode, sweaty as a bronc after a two-mile run, back to Fly's to swab myself off and put on a fresh shirt. The Old Spain, at this time, did not open till five o'clock.

As I pulled my door open, about to leave, another door opened and a man stepped into the hall. As he paused to lock up I noticed the blue serge suit and bowler, and when he turned round I saw he had a large wart on his nose. Been nothing said about warts, but this looked like my chap. "Going to have to ask you to come along and have a talk with the sheriff," I said.

"Sheriff? Who are you?"

"Point is, who are *you*?"

"My name," he said with his chest stuck out like a pouter pigeon's, "is John J. Wriggleston. I'm a watchmaker at Benson, here on business."

"All right, John. Just be a good chap and unbutton that jacket."

When he stood there stiff as a frightened rabbit, I yanked open his coat, and there, sure enough, were the red suspenders. I herded him outside and climbed into my saddle. "Get moving, John. The walk will do you good."

Seventeen

"TOMBSTONE," JOHNNY BEHAN proclaimed as though addressing a student body, "is pretty much of a hybrid, a mining town set down in the midst of vast ranching interests. When the law is mentioned most folks think of the Earps—in particular Wyatt. As the sheriff of Arizona's largest county I have a considerable jurisdiction. I swing a wide loop."

He gave us deputies an impressive look. "I mention this only to set the record straight. There's a lot of law in this town but mostly the apprehension of criminals is left up to me. Jones," he said, "ride over to the Tombstone Mining and Milling and tell them we're holding their Mr. Manley. Someone from there will have to sign a complaint."

"Yes, sir!" Jones said, and left straightaway.

Now Behan turned to the man who called himself Wriggleston and said with a kind of disgust in his look, "Just empty your pockets onto this desk, Manley."

When this had been done he picked up the chap's wallet and extracted from it a considerable sheaf of bank notes—a wad sufficiently large that, if rolled, it would have choked a horse.

"You usually prowl round with this much on your person?"

"I'll have you for false arrest if you don't turn me loose straightaway," declared the man with the wart.

"You haven't been arrested . . . yet," Behan said. "Where did all this currency come from?"

Never blinking an eye, side whiskers bristling, he said with the aplomb of a Boston banker, "I categorically deny your right to question any acts of mine; I deny your right to question *me*, or to restrain me in any fashion, sir!"

Johnny Behan chuckled. "Good show, Manley. You should have been on the stage. Why didn't you run when you had the chance?"

The man drew himself up like an offended Caesar. "I know my rights, sir. I refuse to be intimidated."

A rumble of hoofs clattered up outside, and in through the door swept the irate owner of the Tombstone Mining & Milling Company. Face filled with outrage, he threw on the brakes with such unheralded suddenness young Jones barged into him. He never even noticed. After one sweeping scrutiny: "Where's he at?" he demanded of Behan.

I began to feel sick.

When the sheriff, stiff-faced, thrust a hand out toward the prisoner, the mill owner cried, "That's not my bookkeeper! That feller's not Manley! What the hell kind of law have we got in this county?"

After he'd gone and Wriggleston, overloaded with profuse apologies, had been released and departed, Behan, eyeing me with considerable distaste, said, "Guess I'll have to ask for that badge, Alfred. Afraid you've become a distinct liability."

Eighteen

WHAT COULD I say?

In the face of his embarrassment Behan had every right to send me packing. With an election coming on and politics looming large in his thinking, the sheriff couldn't afford to keep me on. For all he knew that bugger might institute legal proceedings. Probably would if he was who he claimed to be.

I gave him the badge and picked up the check he wrote out for my time. He said, "I'm sorry, Alfred. You done your best and I'm bound to admit that feller had all the earmarks, but you see how it is. Way politics work around here I can't afford you."

So the Last Chance Kid with mouth shut tight went out and climbed into his saddle.

I was sure fed up with the pranks of Fate. From here on out I had the furious resolve to look out for Number One. Good intentions got a man no place. When the chips were down nobody had any use for a loser.

For lack of anything better to do, and with my mood getting blacker with each passing moment, I took off for Galeyville on a hunt for my mare. By God I'd had a bellyful!

There was a wind coming up, blowing hot off the flats, and knowing night would catch up with me long before I could get there, I reckoned to pass the night in the foothills. In between cussing my lousy luck, about all I could think of was that pompous bugger with the wart on his nose.

It was a considerable while before a vision of Josie cut through my fuming. I put her aside as irrelevant right now. The tag I'd facetiously hung on myself back in Broken Butte I'd make my cognomen for none to doubt. The Last Chance Kid was going to make his mark!

In this dangerous mood I rode through the shank of that hot afternoon, at one with the encroaching shadows bending across the trail ahead. If there was symbolism here I failed to see it, taken up as I was with the many aggravations that had been heaped onto me.

Night overtook me at the mouth of Silver Creek Canyon, and I decided not to make a dry camp after all. I picked my way through that faint luminescence with a little more care, mindful of the legs of my horse. The moon came up to hang motionless above me, gilding the brush-choked slopes and cliff sides. The ghostly terrain lay slumbering like something left over from ages long past.

A coyote yapped from a distant ridge, those weird ululations pulsing through the night's quiet like the ripples in water that surround a dropped stone. When I found the right place, I put my horse out of this boulder-strewn wash and up a rugged slope to come out on a spur looking down into the blacker shadows that hemmed Turkey Creek. Not far in that wild tangle below before I'd be sighting the Galeyville mesa, home to the rabble driven out of other places.

Half an hour later, with the moon well down, I dropped into the bottoms beneath ash and sycamore, picking up

in the breeze the wail of a fiddle and the honky-tonk
tinkle of Babcock's piano.

With increased care I put the horse to the grade and
climbed out on the mesa, studying the panels of lamplight
spilling out across the dust of the street from that false-
fronted row of saloons and dance halls whose noise by
now was beginning to wind down just as I remembered
from my stay in that ice house. I'd no way of knowing
if the mare was still here but was determined if she was
to claim her regardless.

Walking my horse past Jack Dall's saloon, I pulled
up and stepped down in front of McCann's, thinking he
might have appropriated Singlefoot in the blame he put
on me on account of Mollie McCarthy.

I looked over the horses tied to his rack, then shoved
through the batwings to confront the stopped talk in a
stillness no louder than a falling leaf. "I've come," I
said bluntly, "to pick up my mare," and searched the
still faces for one bent on trouble. From back of his bar
McCann said gruffly, "You'll not find her here."

"Perhaps you'll oblige by saying where I will."

"I dunno," he growled, having gauged my mood.

Someone else called, "Whyn't you try Babcock's?"

Leaving McCann's, I crossed the street, leading the
horse I'd come on, hearing the mutter of voices behind
me. Singlefoot was tied among others at Babcock's rail
beneath the live oak. She watched me, softly blowing
through distended nostrils.

Reaching out left-handed, I yanked the reins loose.
And just as I did a man stepped out on Babcock's
porch. "What do you think you're doin' over there?"
he demanded.

"Reclaiming my mare. You hunting a piece of this?
A horse thief's the lowest varmint I know."

He stood crouched there a moment, drove a hand at his holster, and just as he touched it, I squeezed the trigger. He went down in a heap. Doors bulged open to reveal wild faces through a curl of black powder smoke drifting between us. No one came out.

With Singlefoot's reins in my left hand, I mounted the horse and, pistol still naked, jogged off toward the Turkey Creek bottoms, leaving them goggling there in Nick's doorway. I reckoned that, like McCann, they had gauged my mood and were happy to see me ride out of the place.

Once out of the mountains, I struck out for Pearce instead of heading for Tombstone. I had thinking to do but was unable to concentrate. A strange kind of lethargy seemed to have come over me. Among my jumbled impressions was one of Josephina; I knew she'd be worried if she found I'd left town, but that I couldn't help.

We continued on, and the moon dropped from sight, and there was nothing to hear but saddle screak and the occasional jingle of spur chains and rowels. A nighthawk sailed past hunting for insects.

Daylight was not far off when I came into the dark huddle of shapes that was Pearce and saw a lone light beckoning. It came from a window of the sorry inn where presumably a night clerk dozed behind his counter. Across the road were the shadow-draped bars of a pole corral, and crossing to it, I got stiffly down, unsaddled both horses, turned them in and tramped back to the paintless hostelry. I flung open the door and pounded the counter till the fellow behind it got sleepily up and shoved out the book for my signature. He dropped a key on the counter. "First room to the left," he said.

I went into the room and locked the door after me, hauled off my boots and sprawled on the bed without bothering to undress.

In the morning I felt more like myself but still a bit groggy as I fished out my timepiece and discovered it to be well after ten. I splashed water on my face, pulled on my boots and slicked back my hair. Picking up my hat, I unlocked the door and walked over to the counter. A different man was back of it now.

Asked where I could find something to eat, he pointed. "Dining room's right through that door if you're not in a hurry." A girl came in an apron presently and I gave her my order. I had steak, eggs, toast and black coffee. After putting these inside me I left some coins on the table and looked through the window at my no-doubt famished horses. At least they had water. I could see the tank from here. A sign down the street spelled LIVERY.

Both horses nickered when I stepped into the sunlit street. I led them, saddled, over to the livery and left them to a feed of oats and hay while I palavered with the proprietor. "Doesn't seem like you'd get many strangers here, being so far off the regular routes."

"Not many," he responded cheerfully. "Where you from?"

"Maybe you like it that way."

"Happens I do. You from Tombstone?"

"That's right."

"One of Behan's deputies? Seems like I recollect your face."

I asked if he'd seen Spence lately.

The liveryman nodded. "Here yesterday." He looked at me awhile. "Come for his horse in the middle of the night. Couldn't hardly wait t'get into the saddle. Friend of yours, is he?"

I smiled. "More like an acquaintance. Don't reckon you noticed which direction he took?"

"Went off towards Steins Pass."

I nodded. "Good stretch of riding with not much between." I rasped at the stubble along my jaw. "Well, thanks," I said.

And he said, "Ain't you the feller chased him onto a train at San Simon a while back?"

"There's a five hundred dollar reward riding on that galoot."

"I swear! What did the little bounder do?"

"Sold me a hotel that didn't belong to him. Stole a horse off Jack McCann."

"That's him, all right." The liveryman grinned. "Pete's bit a lot of folks hither an' yon."

Nineteen

AS YOU MIGHT guess, I was mightily tempted to go after that rascal. But with that kind of start it wasn't likely I'd catch up with him, even with two mounts. Then straight out of the blue I recollected those four letters from London the new man at the Lincoln P. O. had sent back to sender. I put this aside, too; didn't seem so important as it once had.

Time I was getting back, I reckoned. Time to be giving Josie a hand.

Time I got to Charleston I felt the need of wetting my whistle and went into the first saloon I saw. A long, dim room and not much patronage this part of the evening. Off in a corner two cowhands were sitting over drinks. A pair of Cornish miners holding down the far end of the bar. And midway down the mahogany one other man, feller in a blue serge suit and high button shoes pouring ale down his gullet.

The apron fetched me a beer. I shoved it along to where this one was standing. I dropped a hand on his shoulder. "How's the watch business, Wriggleston?"

Jerking free of my hand, he backed off a couple steps looking vastly affronted. "My name's not Wriggleston and I'll thank you to keep your hands off my person."

I grinned. "What name are you going by now, Manley?"

Backing off another step, he regarded me with an outraged glare.

I said, "What happened to your side whiskers and that wart you was wearing last time I talked to you? And that hard hat you was sporting?"

The fellow put his mug on the bar and headed for the doors. Before he could reach them I got hold of his shoulder, spun him around and slammed him against the wall.

The bugger shook a derringer out of his sleeve, and I sent it skittering across the floor. "Time you had another talk with Behan. You can ride in comfort or belly-down across a saddle. Now step outside before I belt you a couple."

He looked around for help without finding any. "Move," I said, and shoved him through the swinging doors.

"Get on that horse," I said, outside. "And don't try to skedaddle or I'll cripple a leg."

Looking pretty ugly, he climbed onto the horse and I swung onto the mare. "All right—get movin'."

The pair of cowhands stood on the porch to watch us ride off. One of them called, "Don't you want that popgun?"

"Keep it," I said, and we headed for Tombstone.

Pulling up in front of Behan's jail, Manley stayed in the saddle till I bade him get down. Young Jones came out with the hard-faced Smith peering over his shoulder. "Boss inside? . . . Good. Ask him to step out here."

Johnny Behan came out looking rather astonished. "This is Thaddeus Manley without his decorations.

Expect he's got something he'd like to discuss with you. Came up with me from Charleston."

"Well?" Behan said, eyeing the fellow sharply.

When Manley just stood there glowering, I said, "Wants to make a clean breast of that business."

Behan looked at me, disgusted. "Farney said—"

"Farney lied. I've got it figured out the pair of them were in cahoots. If this rascal had embezzled that money on his own he'd have been long gone."

Not entirely convinced, the sheriff told Jones to fetch Farney. "Just tell him I want to have a couple words with him."

After the deputy left, Behan asked if Manley wanted to get it off his conscience. The fellow scowled but kept his mouth shut. "Might's well go in and sit down," I suggested.

So we did, Manley looking pretty reluctant but finding no way out of it. Butterfly Smith took up a stance against the door frame, grinning at the captive in a very nasty manner.

A pair of horses pulled up outside. Farney came in; Jones with thumb hooked in shell belt remained in the doorway alongside Smith.

The mill owner's face set like stone when he discovered our guest. The sheriff said, "This is a truth-telling session. That your bookkeeper?"

"No."

"Isn't it true," I said, "that you and him worked up this deal to swindle the company you're insured with?"

Farney kept his mouth shut. Behan said, "Let's see that sheaf of bank notes again."

I smiled at Farney. "Bank will have those serial numbers—"

"All right," Manley growled. "I gave the payroll back

to him. Said he'd pay me my cut when things qui-
eted—"

"You son of a bitch!" Farney made a lunge to get his
hands on the fellow. Before he quite managed, Butterfly
Smith flung him back against the desk. Farney shouted at
Manley, "Don't think you can pin your steal on me!"

"If I get sent up I'm not going alone," Manley muttered. "It was your idea in the first place!"

Sheriff Behan told Smith, "Put them in separate cells.
This is a job for the court—"

Farney's hand drove inside his coat. Butterfly slugged
him. The mill owner reeled back against the desk, where
Jones got the revolver Farney had been reaching for.
Smith, after emptying the mill owner's pockets, hustled
him back to a cell. After the things from Manley's pockets
had joined Farney's belongings on Behan's desk, Jones
prodded the bookkeeper off down the hall and slammed
a cell door on him.

"You know," Behan said to me, "I've a mind to put
you back on the payroll."

"Happens I've already got me a job," I said, and
gave him one of the Old Spain's cards. It read, OLD
SPAIN RESTAURANT—Josephina Maria Vaca y Toro
and Alfred Addlington, Proprietors.

Twenty

JOSEPHINA, WHEN I turned up at the restaurant, showed me one of her brightest smiles. "Oh, Alfie," she said, taking hold of my arm. "I'm so glad you're back. I'm about to wear myself to a nubbin—there don't seem to be enough of me to go round. I'm afraid we're going to have to hire some more help."

"Go ahead. We're doing all right aren't we?"

"Yes, but competent help is hard to find. And I've been thinking . . . a guitar player, plus violin and drummer, could really perk up our profits. And if I was to dance the flamenco once each night . . ."

"Go ahead," I told her. "Sounds like a winner."

"I don't know if we can afford that much new help."

"Let's try it anyhow. I've a chance to play watchman at the Mountain Maid mine—"

"But I was counting on you to stand guard at the cash register . . ."

"Well, there's that girl who used to sing at the Bird Cage, Bannister's wife, Judy. Might be we could get her to do it."

Josie brightened again. "Will you go see if she'll do it?"

"Sure," I said. "And there's that fellow I had in a monkey suit at the Russ House. He'd be all right if we can't get Judy. You get the musicians and I'll see what I can do."

I rode over to Bannister's house. Felt like old times having my saddle back on Singlefoot. I looked through my wallet, which was a lot less fat than I liked to see it. Judy came to the door. I broached the matter of the job. "Oh, I'd love to," she said, "but Arlie wouldn't stand for it. He thinks a man's wife belongs in the home."

I went hunting for the doorman I'd employed at the Russ House. Took me till dark, but I finally found him working as a swamper at the Alhambra Saloon.

"You kiddin'?" he said, and grinned when I told him what I'd come for.

"Straight goods," I said, "but you'll have to spruce up a bit. You still got that monkey suit?"

"You bet! When do I start?"

"Be there tomorrow afternoon about four."

This settled, I rode up to the Mountain Maid and went into the office alongside the hoist. Man back of the desk looked up and said, "Yes?"

"Sheriff said you're hunting an honest man to play watchdog."

He pushed back his eyeshade and looked me over. "Ain't you kind of on the peaked side? I been thinking of a huskier man. What have you done?"

"Broke broncs, worked in a livery, rode for Burt Mossman, been one of Behan's deputies—"

"Why'd you leave Behan?"

"Decided I wasn't cut out for a deputy. Figured the grass might look greener someplace else."

He looked me over some more. "This job," he said, still dubious, "could get you killed. We got problems here. On top of havin' to put in a change room to keep the best ore from sproutin' wings, the last week or so somebody's sticky fingers has been at my amalgam. Them stage robbings is gettin' so prevalent I'm scared to ship. I'll have to run a check on you."

"That's okay."

"What do I call you?"

"Alfred Addlington." I handed him one of the Old Spain cards. He showed more interest. "Hmm," he said. "All right, I'll take a chance on you."

"When do I start?"

"Be here at four-thirty tomorrow afternoon."

I rode back to Fly's and toted up my finances. Total cash in hand came to three hundred and eighty-four dollars, disregarding the change. Back at the American Hotel I told Josie about getting that doorman to sit at the register. "And I got that job at the Mountain Maid." Then I put my three hundred and eighty-four dollars into her hand. "This might help a little."

"Oh, Alfie! Can you afford it?"

"What are partners for?" I grinned. "Might have to take meals here for a spell." She leaned toward me. "Of course," she said, wrinkling her nose at me. "You can eat here anytime. What's this new fellow's name?"

"Call him Geoffrey—for what we're paying he'll answer to anything. Isn't that a new girl waiting on tables?"

"Yes—Dolores, and you keep away from her!"

Next day at around three-thirty I rode over to the Mountain Maid and reported for duty. The man said, "Behan's okayed you. Called you impulsive but honest and bright. Told me he hated to lose you. Come along and I'll show you the change room and where we're keepin' the amalgam."

I followed him around without introductions. "New man," he mentioned to the others. To me he said, "Shift comes up right after five and twenty minutes later a new shift goes down, working till five in the morning. You're on your own," he grunted, and went back to the office.

He had an assayer who worked days in a small adobe back of the office, about one hundred feet to the left of the change room. I looked over this last place carefully but came up with no hidden ore. I was sure those boys wouldn't bother with anything but jewelry rock. Ore thieves around here were known as *gambesinos*—might not have spelled that right, never having seen it in print. Then I went back to the assayer's shack. There was a strong room built in at one end of this place, of oak planks with a solid oak door three inches thick, I was told, and secured by a heavy padlock.

"How long," I asked, "has this padlock been on here?"

"Couple weeks. Gets changed tomorrow," the assayer said.

"Who keeps the keys?"

"The owner. Right in his pocket."

"What time do you get off work?"

"Soon's the shift comes up."

"You keep the door of this place locked?"

"With two windows? What's the use? Guard they used to have slept most of the night here."

I looked around. "Whereabouts?"

"On that foldin' cot. Right up against the strong room door."

"Must have taken two men to lift him out of the way. Wonder he didn't wake up."

"Guess he had better sense," the assayer said.

I thought about that. Fellow could be right. "How much have they been grabbing?"

"Went off with the whole works last time."

I whistled. "Big temptation. Be cheaper to ship it. They can't be stopping every stage that goes out."

"No. Only the profitable ones."

"When was the last time?"

"Just before they put on this padlock." He said with a snort, "You ever hear of a burglarproof padlock?"

"Looks pretty stout."

The fellow's lip curled. "I could open that door in less than two minutes!"

"Go ahead."

"It ain't me that's been liftin' that stuff."

"Didn't figure it was. Go ahead—show me."

"All you got to do is bend back that hasp an' take out the screws. Kid could do it."

"Is that how they get in?"

"Used a key last time. I told him if he wants to stop this stealin' to keep a man with a gun in here overnight. A feller with guts enough to use it."

"If it's someone coming off the day shift," I said, "I better stay right here where they'll not get a look at me. What time's the owner leave?"

"Soon's this shift has gone through the change room—likes to keep an eye on 'em."

"I'll be staying right here till this shift goes back in the mine tomorrow. If that lock gets changed tomorrow and no one gets in here tonight it will be a couple days before they can get a new key made. First off they'll have to get an impression."

He nodded. "Happy dreams. I'm headin' for home."

There weren't many places in here a man could hide. I saw an old tarp folded up in a corner which I thought some of nailing across the strong room door. It wouldn't do much good if they had a knife. I put the cot against the door and loaded it down with all the junk I could find. Then I shook out the tarp, sat down against the wall and pulled it over me.

I reckoned in the dark this would hide me nicely, but I'd have to stay under it, boots, head and all—be awful damn hot. I got out my pocket knife and cut me a little slit for my eyes, pulled the tarp back over me. Five minutes was sufficient to bring out the sweat. I put my head outside again. If they didn't show up I'd be limp as a dishrag by morning.

Time dragged slower than a long-winded sermon. For a while various notions kept my mind reasonably busy. I felt lonelier in here than I ever remembered being. It wasn't yet dark, and it seemed pretty certain no thieves would show up before midnight at the soonest. I got out from under that goddam tarp, blew out my breath and eventually cooled off some. And about that time the shadows began to thicken up.

Kind of odd the sort of things a chap will come up with when his hands are idle and nothing to occupy his mind. I wondered if I was ever mentioned at Turkey Track, and how Higgins and his taffy-haired daughter were getting along at Broken Butte. And where that damn Pete Spence had got to. I even wondered a bit about that hard-cased Butterfly Smith taken on to replace Dry Camp. Strange pick for a sheriff, it seemed like.

Took a long time to get dark. Be longer still before another day dawned. I wondered what Josephina was doing and if the ex-doorman from the Russ House had showed up as promised.

As night inched down and the quiet piled up, it became a chore just to keep my eyes propped open. Half a dozen times I caught myself dozing off. My shirt felt like it was stuck to my back, and a near unbearable cramp—a charley horse probably—had hold of one leg, and I was minded to throw off that tarp and get up.

And finally I did, staring into the dark, well back from the windows. A low-turned lamp, in the office evidently, threw a pale bar of light across motionless shadows. Made me wonder if the boss for some reason had come back to work late; I got to wondering, too, if it was somebody else over there . . .

Pistol in hand, I got back under the tarp, determined to ward off sleep, and must have dozed despite myself for of a sudden I was wide awake, listening, with nothing to hear but the thud of my heart.

Then sound came again, the screak of dry hinges as the door was eased open. Against the lighter outside dark I watched the shapes of two men edging cautiously through it, stealthily moving toward the strong room door, and wished I'd thought to fetch that cut-down shotgun. An explosive grunt, a smothered curse. One of them, I reckoned, had banged a shin against that cot I'd loaded with rocks and scrap iron. A match flared briefly in a cupped hand as they stood glaring.

As it was snuffed and dropped, the larger of the two said, "We're goin' to have to move it—catch hold of that other end. Take it over by that bench. Sure you've got that key?"

"You think I'm a nump? 'Course I've got it. Come on, let's git that door open."

"I got the feelin' somebody's watchin' us," the shorter one whispered, twisting his head around.

They'd got the cot moved out of the way and were back in front of the padlocked door, a pair of crouched shapes, not much darker than the enveloping murk. The short one bent to fetch the key from his shoe. I could hear the sharp click as the padlock was sprung, saw them step back as the door was pulled open.

Another match was struck as they moved into the strong room and tested the weight of the wooden chest I could see between them. "Pretty good haul," the bigger one muttered. The match went out. I pictured them bending over the chest. They came staggering out with it. While they both still had hold of it, I said, "Just take it on outside," and threw off the tarp to come bounding erect, pistol in hand.

The pair stood frozen for perhaps a couple seconds. The smaller one then let go of his grip, and everything seemed to happen at once as he reached for his shooter and the bigger one yelled as that chest slammed into him and I squeezed trigger.

They were both down now, the bigger one cursing as he tried to get loose of that heavy chest, which had one of his legs pinned against the concrete floor. "You'll only make it worse," I growled, sharp-eyed to make sure he hadn't a gun in his fist. When I was pretty sure he hadn't, I struck a match and put flame to the lamp hanging from the rafters above the bench.

Bending, I grabbed the shooter from his holster, got the smaller robber's too, wondering how long the fellow would last with a bullet through his lungs and the wheeze of them making that awful sound as the blood piled up inside him.

Putting their guns on the bench and my own where it had come from, I stood eyeing the man pinned down by the chest. "If I move it," I told him, "it's going to hurt worse than hell because I can't lift it off you. All I can do is drag it."

"Don't drag it fer Gawd's sake," he gasped between groans.

Wasn't much I could do for the other one, either. Could have torn up his shirt and wrapped it over the hole, but with so little blood coming out, this would just be an exercise in futility.

I walked over to the door and looked outside, saw the three saddled horses tied to the hitch rail, one of them in a pack saddle with burlaps to put the loot in. I came back and sat down on the stool by the bench. Not much I could do but wait for some help while listening to the groans of the man with the smashed leg.

Dawn finally outlined the eastern hills, and shortly thereafter the day shift began arriving in twos and threes and, seeing the hitched horses, congregated outside until the shift boss arrived and herded them over to the hoist.

The assayer came bustling into his workshop. "Bagged 'em, eh?" he exclaimed, eyeing the prostrate pair. The man with the pinned leg had passed out; the smaller one was conscious but in no shape for comment. "Want I should help you get the chest off that feller?"

"Another few minutes won't make much difference."

"By God, you're a cool one!" He stared at me with what looked like mixed feelings. "How long's that chest been anchorin' him there?"

"Couple hours I guess."

The Mountain Maid's owner, having seen the tied horses, came hustling in. "What are them horses—" He broke off, his widening stare taking in the pair on the floor. "Here, one of you give me a hand with that chest."

"Better wait," I said, "till the sheriff's had a look at this."

He eyed me a moment then sent the assayer off on one of the horses to fetch Behan. "And tell him to fetch a wagon for these fellers." With a final look at the casualties, he went off to his office.

Johnny Behan arived with a wagon and both deputies. He listened to my account while young Jones and Butter-fly Smith manhandled the chest back into the strong room and padlocked the door. Jones handed me the key looking properly impressed; then he and Smith on the sheriff's instructions loaded the robbers into the bed of the wagon and the driver took off in the direction of the hospital.

Behan considered me awhile with an enigmatic stare and presently with a shrug went off to palaver with the Mountain Maid's owner.

"Fine mare you've got there," declared the assayer while removing his hat and donning his green eyeshade. He sat down at his bench to begin his day's work.

Going outside, I swung into the saddle and headed for town.

Twenty-One

LAST NIGHT WHILE waiting for those chaps to show up I'd had time enough to have a look at where I was headed, and a number of notions had caught at my attention. For one thing it appeared I was too fond of change, new scenes, jobs and faces. Fiddle-footed, it looked like; a man with no roots, going from day to day with no real plan or purpose.

For years I'd dreamed of being a cowboy. Thanks to Mossman's range boss I'd gotten a start to becoming a top hand, but hadn't stayed with it. I was beginning to suspect this wasn't just fiddle-footedness. I seemed to be attracted to turmoil; it was the possibility of action that seemed to rivet my attention. Getting ahead in the world had not appeared to hold much interest I was surprised to discover.

Perhaps I lacked the acquisitive instinct.

Beginning to feel like a misfit, I headed for my lodgings at Fly's Boarding House.

Killing that fellow didn't bother me a heap. I wondered if I was one of those cut out to be a gunslinger, and found the thought repugnant. Getting right down to it I didn't seem to have been taking much pleasure in anything. Except, it now confronted me, in Josephina, who claimed to have been the progeny of a cow and a bull. I grinned at the whimsy, not much caring what she had sprung from. I discovered that I liked most everything about her, all that is but her pushy ways. I had a deep-seated aversion to being managed. And she was a manager, no doubt of that.

Still wondering if I could put up with that, I scrubbed myself, put on a fresh shield-fronted shirt and slicked down my hair. Back in the saddle I headed for the restaurant, still wondering what it would be like having her to come home to.

She was an odd sort of girl, not that I'd known many others. I recalled how quickly she had captivated Farsom; I'd always reckoned Flick to be a love-'em-and-leave-'em sort of cove, but he had sure been mighty interested in her.

How long would I be content to settle down I wondered. If I married Josie, could I make a go of it? She was exciting, a tumultuous personality; I reckoned life with her wouldn't ever be dull. She was well put together, lithe and passionate, quick to fly into a temper, a good head on her shoulders and fun to be with . . .

All this exploring into such unaccustomed notions turned me restless and jumpy. Seemed like I was at some sort of crossroads. I had a desperate need to know where I was going, and this didn't make much sense to me either. I never had wondered about such things before.

I rode around for a while, up one street and down another, pushing around the things in my head and still not able to figure what ailed me. I presently discovered myself outside the hotel, got down, tossed Singlefoot's reins across the rack, went inside and down the hall and entered our eating place knowing, from a glance at my timepiece, Josie would likely be up to her ears in the last-minute chores that seemed always to herald the opening of the doors.

The outside entrance hadn't yet been opened. I could see Geoffrey standing there, watch in hand. I decided to come round later. Back on the street I got into my saddle and, returning to my room at Fly's, took to pacing the floor, aggravated beyond what I found to be acceptable. I knew this was something I'd got to come to grips with. A half hour's pacing brought no solution.

A blur of motion beyond the window caught at my attention.

To the west of my room was a deep vacant lot. There was one small dwelling at its far western boundary where it intersected Fremont Street. Just this side of that private house several men with horses were grouped in a huddle, watching the street in an attitude of waiting.

I recognized all five: Billy Clayborne, Ike Clanton, Tom McLaury, Billy Clanton and Frank McLaury with a hand on his saddle horn. There was something about them that held me staring without knowing why.

Just as Frank lifted a boot to stirrup, I glimpsed what I guessed this bunch had been waiting for. Half a block away four grim-faced men rounded into Fremont and came striding toward Fly's. These fellows were Wyatt Earp, Doc Holiday with a shotgun, Virgil Earp, who was town marshal, and Morgan Earp.

Sensing trouble, I couldn't have been dragged away from that window.

I knew these two factions nursed a long-standing antagonism and by all the signs and signal smokes appeared to be heading for a showdown.

The Clantons and McLaurys, heavily armed and with patience apparently exhausted, were about to climb into their saddles when the Earps and Doc Holiday came into their sight. Wyatt Earp and Frank McLaury fired simultaneously. I heard the roar of Holiday's shotgun and saw Tom McLaury buckle against the telegraph pole. The racket of gunfire was thrown back from the buildings. My window shook. Clayborne and Ike Clanton dashed for cover behind Fly's building. Morgan Earp was down, writhing in the dust, gun still blasting at Frank McLaury, who, already hit, was staggering along toward the north side of Fremont. Billy Clanton had blood on wrist and chest. He'd slumped down by the private home above mentioned. In less than thirty seconds the whole thing was over, the air still ringing with the echo of gunshots.

I jerked away from the window, thinking to run down there but, getting a grip on myself, sat down on the bed to think this over. Looked like to me there'd be hell to pay. This feud had certainly been festering for weeks. Both factions had friends and plenty of enemies. I was reminded of Lincoln and the feuding over there. I'd got out of that one, got clean away from it, and had no hankering to get mixed up in this. Another odd quirk in the character of one who appeared to thrive on violence. Maybe, I thought, I was beginning to grow out of it. Perhaps getting a modicum of sense at long last.

I was still in my room when a knock at the door a short while later brought me onto my feet. "Come in," I said with hand at belt.

It was Johnny Behan with his face in grim lines. "You hear about that street fight?"

I nodded. "Here when it happened. I saw the whole thing. What touched it off?"

He shoved a fist along his jaw. "The Clantons and McLaurys had been warned some time ago not to come into town wearing guns. Some damn fool—I'm not sure who—came busting to Wyatt to say those fellows were looking for trouble."

"How many of them died?"

"Frank and Tom McLaury and Billy Clanton. Virgil and Morgan Earp were wounded."

"What are you figuring to do about it?"

Behan said uneasily, "I suppose I shall have to arrest the survivors." He ran worried eyes over me. "I had just come into the back of that lot when the shooting started. I'm not at all sure what I saw."

"You see Clayborne and Ike Clanton duck out of it?"

"I saw them run into this building." He eyed me some more. "You wouldn't be hankering to pin a badge on again?"

"No I wouldn't. I've had enough violence."

"I could sure use another deputy . . ."

"Well, don't look at me."

After he left I rode back to the restaurant. I felt the need of a talk with Josephina. Geoffrey opened the door and invited me into the fan-cooled interior. "Ask the boss if she can step out here a moment."

She came out straightaway, taking my hands with that gamine grin. "Is this something you'd like to say privately?"

When I nodded she led me into the coat room, a small cubicle off the entrance hall. She closed the door, saying, "What did you wish to speak about, Alfred?"

"Us," I said, and pawed at my face, finding it hard to get started.

She said, "Yes?" as if to give me encouragement. "I'm all attention."

"Would . . . ah—what do you think about marrying me?"

I did not think she was particularly surprised. Nor, as I'd been hoping, did she fling her arms around me. Her direct regard considered me with an intensity I had not expected. "What brought this up?"

"I been thinking," I said kind of lame-like.

"Well, that's something new."

I said, not entirely free from resentment, "I thought you liked me."

"That's right. I do. More than you imagine. But I don't think you're ready for marriage yet, Alfie."

"You don't? Why not?" I said, startled.

"For one thing . . . that job at the Mountain Maid."

"What's that have to do with it? Anyhow, I'm giving that up—had to shoot a man last night."

"So you're giving it up. Don't you see, Alfie? You've given up a lot of jobs. I don't believe you're ready to settle down . . . take up responsibilities. When I get married it will be to someone I can depend on—"

"Flick Farsom, I reckon."

"No. He's another like you. Hasn't grown up yet."

Seeing my anger, she smiled at me sadly. "A grown-up person knows what he wants, is willing to make a real effort to get it. I can't believe you know what you want."

"If I didn't want you I wouldn't have asked you," I said, stung into saying more than I'd intended.

Her eyes never wavered. "There's a lot of good in you, Alfie, but I've knocked around enough to want a good provider. You're too much of a butterfly for me to feel we could make a go of it."

She lifted a hand when I opened my mouth. "Hear me out. All things considered, this place is doing well. But without we can get hold of a large chunk of cash, this new help will have to go before another month's out because we're not taking in enough to pay them and have anything left for ourselves."

Again, when I would have spoken, she said, "Let me finish. I have a small mine. I think I've mentioned it before. It's a placer. On a stream about ten miles from Broken Butte. Up in the hill country. If you'll go there and work it and come in once a month with whatever you've found—and still want to marry me, we'll talk it over again."

Twenty-Two

OUTSIDE I SAID to Singlefoot, "There's gratitude for you!" and got into the saddle. Inside my shaken self I was finding those home truths hard to digest. Nobody cares to hear his failures spelled out, more especially by a chit of a girl! Resentment had all my nerves in a jangle, and it was like I was still in short pants on leading strings, and I went out of there looking for a dog I could kick.

I felt bad in need of a drink right then and got off my mare at the Crystal Palace and shoved through the batwings with blood in my eye. And the first face I saw was Billy's—that damn little horse thief Farsom had long made out to be hunting. "Well," he said. "Damn if it ain't that Last Chance bugger I run out of Lincoln! Git outa my way," he said with curled lip.

Stopped square in his path, I said without caution, "Not till you've paid that hundred bucks you swindled me out of at Seven Oaks for that stolen horse you palmed off on me."

His look turned ugly as galvanized sin, but I didn't budge so much as an inch.

He jounced to a stop, turning black as a thundercloud. "Git outa my way 'fore I blow you into the middle of next week!"

"The bigger the mouth . . . Well, you know what they say. I'm not moving till you pay up."

The place grew quiet with hung-up breaths, the bunch around us expecting an explosion while Billy stood with every bristle jittering. Then this terrible goblin pawed at his face with that pale stare looking like clouded glass. He pulled out his roll and peeled off five twenties, which he flung on the floor at my feet with a snarl.

"Pick them up, hardcase, and put them in my hand."

You'd have given odds it wouldn't ever happen, but after another wild look he did just that. Shoving them into a pocket, I walked out of the place, drink forgotten, suddenly thankful to be alive.

You can see how far good intentions went. I got into the saddle with knees like rubber and, cutting through alleys, went back to the restaurant, my mind made up that from here on out I would take no guff from anyone.

In front of the Old Spain I was seized by another notion and forked my mare to the Mountain Maid, hoping to catch the owner before he set out for home. He was still in the office. I put the strong room key right in front of him on his desk and told him I'd come to pick up my time.

He looked astonished. "You're quitting?"

"Don't reckon you'll need me here any longer. I'm bound for a job near Broken Butte. I'll be doing some mining."

"You can mine right here if that's what you're wanting."

"Not the same," I said. "I'll be a partner up there."

"Well, good luck." He put a ten dollar bill down alongside the key.

"That's more than we bargained for."

"Take it—you've earned it."

So I picked it up and went back to the restaurant. The place was open, every table filled, with Geoffrey in his monkey suit perched on a stool where Flick Farsom used to sit. I put the five twenties on the ledge by the register. "When she comes to tote up tonight you can tell her I've gone to Broken Butte."

It proved a three-day ride. I got in one evening just short of dark, took a room at the hotel, a little surprised to find Dixie Higgins still back of the counter. "Hello there, cowboy," she exclaimed with a smile. "Where have you been?"

"About half a jump from the Mexican border. How's tricks with you?"

"Been considerably better since El Miga's departure." Her arms came up and crossed her breasts. "Your money's no good here you know—we don't charge friends."

"The sure road to bankruptcy."

"We don't have that many," she said with a laugh. "Our best friend around here is Armagón Posada. Seems he'd no idea of the way that feller was carrying on."

"Room four?" I said when she handed me the key.

"It's a tiny bit nicer than the room you had last time."

I guessed, looking round, it was the best in the house. I had a good night's sleep, at peace with myself. For the moment anyway.

The mine or claim, from what Josie'd told me, was about ten miles from town. I had no trouble in following her directions, finding each landmark in its right place. I found the stream with that unpronounceable Indian name and high rock ledges both sides of the canyon. She had patented her claim, strictly a placer operation, and I'd come for a look before laying in supplies.

I got into the canyon about the middle of the morning and had not gone far before the sound of voices told me someone was working it. I could hear the swishing sound of gravel in a rocker. Just around the next bend was where her claim ought to be—where the sounds were coming from. I'd fetched my shotgun, and while I considered the situation I made sure both barrels were loaded.

I eased the mare forward, rounded the bend, and there they were, a pair of husky rascals, sleeves rolled up and standing in rubber hip boots, one of them leaning on a long-handled shovel while the other looked over what they'd caught in the rocker.

I said, "Getting much?"

They both whirled, startled. The one reaching beltward spied the sawed-off and froze. "What's it to you?" growled the one with the shovel.

"Since I'm repping for the owner I'd be interested to know."

The shovel man turned ugly. "You're lookin' at the owner. Now get out of here!"

"What I'm looking at," I said, "are a pair of claim jumpers. Just empty your pockets into that rocker and be on your way."

They had put up a tent, and their horses were grazing off back of it I saw as they were making up their minds what to do about me. The shovel man said, "You've either got the wrong crick or the wrong location. You'll find our names in that corner marker. We been workin' this claim for the past six months."

"Must have piled up quite a stake in that time," I remarked. "Fetch it out and I'll figure what I owe you for labor. That way we can part with no hard feelings."

This was giving them an out, letting them off lightly, but they weren't the kind to let well enough alone. While I appeared engrossed with the man holding the shovel, the other one reckoned to sneak out a gun and empty my saddle. I loosed a charge from the right-hand barrel. It caught him square in the chest, driving him back. With knees going limber he dropped limp as an emptied sack, half doubled over, into that foot-deep gurgling stream.

I said to the shovel holder's bugged-out stare, "I've another barrel here I'm saving for you. Get rid of the iron you've got on your hip—throw the whole works, belt and all, in the water."

When this was done I said, "Take your shovel and go dig him a grave—off there someplace out of the way." He looked pretty sick but went off to start digging, and while he was at it, I got the other one's pistol, which I stuck in my waistband.

The shoveler had the shakes so bad it took the best part of half an hour to get his friend buried. Then, dripping sweat and pale as wood ash, he stood watching me nervously.

I said, "Go empty your pockets like I told you before that fellow got careless." When this was done I bade him take his horse and get lost in a hurry. "If I see you again I'm shooting on sight."

I guessed by his look he was glad to clear out. Since I'd already lifted the rifle off his saddle, it didn't seem likely he'd be back for some while. I took my gear off the mare and turned her loose to graze with the other horse. Then I picked over the stuff in the rocker. About the only thing to come out of his pockets that was worth hanging onto was the contents of his wallet, four hundred in bank notes and a couple of letters addressed to Buck Baldwin, Esquire, care of General Delivery,

Broken Butte, Arizona. I shoved the currency in my pocket and chucked the rest of his stuff in the creek, watching it sail downstream out of sight.

Caught in the rocker were about a hundred dollars' worth of nuggets. These I scooped into my hat for the moment and walked over to see what they had in the tent.

I threw out the two sleeping bags and the dead man's saddle after relieving it of his Winchester. The ground was packed hard enough to show they'd been here a month at least. I took a look at their supplies—about enough for three days with only myself to feed. I picked up the shovel, buried the saddle and sleeping bags, then dug up the floor of the tent.

In an hour's work I turned up a small sack filled with gold dust and two coffee cans filled with nuggets, a total value of about twelve hundred dollars. Next I fished through the claim's markers till I found their fraudulent notice. I destroyed it and wrote up one naming Josephina as owner.

With their loot carefully stored in my saddle bags, I climbed into the saddle, and with the dead man's horse in tow, I headed for Tombstone, destroying the rocker before I left.

Twenty-Three

THERE SEEMED A pretty good chance the man I'd let go would round up some cronies and be back, aiming to bury me. He could probably do it if he fetched enough help. What I needed in addition to a month's supplies was a knocked-down sluice and, at least, another helper. And it wouldn't be smart to acquire these at Broken Butte. The farther I stayed from that place the better.

I rode with the shotgun across my pommel and a claim-jumper's Winchester beneath my left leg.

Having continued through a good piece of the night, I made a dry camp to give Singlefoot a rest, hid the saddle in some hillside brush, and chased off the dead man's mount. Well before sunup I was back on the mare, again pointed south. When I made a second night's camp I had covered about two-thirds of my journey, with Tombstone less than twenty miles away.

Adding the nuggets I'd taken from the rocker to those I had found in the two coffee cans, I had by conservative count at least thirteen hundred dollars to turn over to Josephina. Which would probably, I thought, keep her going till I could get her some more.

This second layover was of short duration, just long enough to let the mare browse awhile and rest up a little. I aimed to reach town before daylight, and did, leaving

Singlefoot at Dunbar's stable, along with her saddle, the shotgun and rifle.

With the saddle bags over my shoulder, I hoofed it to my room at Fly's and stretched out on my bed. I slept the whole morning and half the afternoon. After washing the dust and sweat off and treating myself to a hasty shave, I put on fresh clothes and set out to find Fly.

I finally ran him down at his business address and left the nuggets secured in a canvas sack, which I told him Josephina would be around to pick up. Leaving him, I walked over to the establishment that supplied our groceries, bought enough grub and staples for a week's stay at the claim, putting them on our bill for the restaurant, and told them this stuff was to go in two burlaps that I'd call for later.

Next I went over to Dunbar's to pick up my mare and a couple of pack mules with sawhorse saddles, which I charged to the restaurant. I got onto my mare and, leading the mules, rode over to the Old Spain to put a feed under my belt. It was then six o'clock and the place was half-filled.

Sitting down at a table for two in the corner nearest the kitchen, I told Dolores what I wanted to eat and to let Josephina know where I was sitting. She came out straightaway. "Sit down and catch your breath," I said.

"Alfie—what is it? Why are you back?"

So I gave her the gist of what I'd found at her claim. "The nuggets," I said, "I've left with Fly—you can pick them up whenever you want them." And she said, looking worried, "That one you drove off . . . do you think he'll come back?"

"It wouldn't surprise me, if he can round up some help."

For the next several minutes, lip caught between teeth,

she studied me anxiously. "I don't think you ought to go back there alone."

"I want to look that place over more carefully. If it appears good enough to afford a helper I'll get one. The prime object right now is to keep this place going and, if we're lucky, build up a nest egg. Don't worry, I'll keep my eyes skinned. Meanwhile I want you to get me a sluice. Some place that sells mining timbers can take care of that. I'll want it made so it can be broken down and packed. I'll be back in ten days; it should be ready by that time. We'll pay for it out of what I bring back."

Three days later I was back on that stream with a gold pan, some ore sacks and the canned stuff and staples I'd fetched on the mules. I'd left my shotgun at Fly's, replaced it with a Sharps, which could knock down a buffalo at four hundred yards. I'd also brought along the Winchester I'd inherited from the claim-jumper I'd shot. The other fellow's rifle I'd smashed on a rock and thrown into the stream a couple hundred feet below where I was working. I'd brought enough shells to stand off a mob.

First of all I wanted to see what we had here. I hobbled the two mules but left Singlefoot loose. There was enough browse around to keep all three of them happy. Nothing had changed apparently while I'd been gone; no sign of any further intrusions. I walked up the canyon for a good half mile, finding no fresh tracks. On the way back I examined the streambed as well as I was able, found a series of pools that I believed would pay working.

I put my supplies in the tent. Coyotes or bobcats had dug up the sleeping bags; I burned what was left of them. At first light next morning I got to work, moving upstream a ways in the hip boots I'd fetched. The nuggets were being carried from somewhere above, a good piece like enough, for I found color wherever I panned. Each try at a pool I found a few nuggets as I worked back toward camp. .

I opened a tall can of tomatoes, drank the juice and ate the pulp. I waded into the pool above where the robbers had been working. The stream at this point wasn't as deep and maybe five feet wider than the ten-foot width Josephina had staked. A good quantity of nuggets appeared to be lodged in the silt below boulders and a lot more in the ripples above them. This shallow pool was easier to work in. I went back to camp, got the pick and worked some of the smaller rocks out of the streambed, stacking them along the downside edge in a kind of baffle, which increased the sound of gurgling water. I figured in time this would pile up more nuggets coming down from above.

I went back to the tent through the lengthening shadows and cooked some supper, using for fuel only bits and pieces of dead wood to keep down the smoke, it not being my intention to advertise my presence. There was no way of knowing who might be prowling these hills. There was plenty of riffraff hanging out around Broken Butte, scarcely ten miles away.

I hung a nosebag of oats on each of my animals, ate my own supper, washed up after me and went early to bed. When I got up next morning I had an abundance of aching muscles from such unaccustomed labor. I reckoned yesterday's efforts would net about eight hundred dollars. A pretty good day's pay. Better than several months of working for Behan.

The mules and Singlefoot weren't far away. Making a tiny fire, I cooked up some breakfast, which I enjoyed beyond normal. I was just washing up when Singlefoot nickered. I picked up the Sharps and got braced for company. I caught an answering nicker and, a moment later, discovered a solitary rider rounding the bend.

He gave me a hail, and I was some astonished to recognize Jones, Behan's youngest deputy. He rode into camp and sat looking down at me. "Hoped to come up with you yesterday." He grinned. Got directions from Miz Josie. Judge Barnes is holding District Court in Tombstone two weeks from now and Sheriff wants you back to give testimony against Dry Camp and those three stage robbers you captured."

"How about giving you my affidavit?"

"I got orders to fetch you back."

"Hellsfire! I've got all I can handle right now right here."

"Can't help it," he said. "I got my orders."

"You figuring to throw a gun on me?"

Jones grinned. "Not likely."

"Well, it ain't convenient for me to go back now—"

"Don't have to leave this minute," he said. "Reckon you can work another four, five days an' still git back in plenty of season. I'll stay here till you're ready to go."

"All right," I muttered, matching his grin. "You've talked me into it. You'll have to work for your keep though. You any good with a shovel?"

He got down off his horse. "I'm ready," he said. "Where do I start?"

"Get that horse hobbled first of all."

"No need," he said. "Like me, this horse comes from timid stock—won't let me out of his sight if he can help it. Let me get that saddle an' bridle off so he can roll an' he'll be happy as a lark."

"Just one thing," I told him. "When we leave this

place whatever you've seen you keep to yourself—understood? I've enough on my plate without standing off stampeders."

"I got a lock on my jaw." He peered round curiously. He had no wading boots, but I found plenty for him to do. We worked that pool all day, straight through, taking out between us more than nine hundred dollars' worth of nuggets, several of them big around as marbles. We knocked off then, went back to camp and filled our bellies.

The following day, still working the same pool, we nearly doubled that amount. "Gosh," Jones said, "this is more fun than anything I've done."

"If we had a fine-toothed rake we could be millionaires in about three days. Let me get in there with this pick and stir it up."

When I'd climbed out and put on my shirt, we took the day's catch back to the tent and put it away with the rest of the nuggets. "If this keeps up," Jones laughed, "you will soon be too rich to talk to anyone but mine owners."

Next morning, soon as we'd gobbled our breakfast, we were back and hard at it. In the past couple days the muck we'd shoveled out had raised the water level almost to the tops of my boots. We piled more rocks behind our baffle in an attempt to increase the amount of gold we were trapping.

"If we could divert the stream—take it around this pool—I believe," Jones said, "we could get at this better. It's all this silt washing down from above! Keeps buryin' them. If we can stop the silt we would find more nuggets."

Leaning on the shovel, studying the intake, I nodded. "I reckon that's right. We'll try it tomorrow."

Twenty-Four

WHEN WE FINALLY knocked off to go back to the tent it seemed like we'd gathered a pretty fair haul. I took care of the oats for the mules and Jones took care of the horse he had come on. After we'd eaten we dug out the nuggets we'd been sacking, added what we had picked up today and stared at each other in gratified surprise. As Jones remarked, seemed like we'd better than four thousand dollars' worth. "Biggest problem," he said, "with wealth of this sort, it don't have no serial numbers."

It was anyone's gold who was able to hang onto it. The problem this posed was easy to see, finding a solution looked like being more difficult. No good burying it under the tent. If that sod I'd let go came back with help, they'd have it dug up in no time at all.

We had put out our fire, and young Jones suggested the best place to hide the gold was under the ashes.

It was getting dark fast, and as we stepped from the tent, Jones with the sacked gold under one arm and me with the shovel, the hat was ripped from my head and Jones let out a yell that sounded like hell emigrating on cartwheels.

I dropped flat, letting go of the shovel. Jones, nearby and sprawled at full length, was twisting his head as though his neck were made of India rubber. "They're up on high ground, only reason we ain't both of us dead already!" I reckoned he was right; firing downhill, you're inclined to shoot high.

From where I'd dropped, our rifles were just out of reach. "Keep down," I muttered, and wriggled back far enough to get a hand on that single-shot buffalo gun. Both Winchesters, repeaters, might just as well have been in Nogales for all the good they were like to do, being a long six feet away. I said in a whisper, "Don't move a muscle. Let 'em think we're finished. They might get careless."

One of the intruders certainly did. Against that dark hillside I caught a brief glimpse of motion as a blacker shadow fractionally moved. I waited, sweating, for it to move again. When it did I fired. In the blur of commotion Jones got inside the tent. "Get down you fool!" I growled at him. He barely had as a volley of shots brought the tent down on top of us, snapping its center pole.

"Here," he grunted, wriggling out of its folds, and shoved a Winchester against my elbow. "They're up on that ridge."

"They'll be spreading out directly. Don't fire blind— wait for a target." I was watching those flashes. "Doubt if there's more than three of them up there." Meanwhile I'd got the Sharps reloaded. Jones, pushing his Winchester ahead of him, was wriggling off toward a boulder he was hoping to get back of.

"Let 'em have it!" someone yelled, and muzzle lights flashed again from the dark, and in the midst of this racket I squeezed trigger, the voice of that Sharps drowning even Jones's firing and the ricochets of slugs whining round us. "This kind of thing could go on all night," I muttered, disgusted.

But there were no more shots.

"They've pulled out," Jones growled after a while, and brashly stood up. But nothing happened, so I got up myself. He said, impatient, "Let's go find—"

"We'll find out in the morning. Going up there now could be just what they're waiting for."

I hadn't heard any sounds of departure, but they could have led their horses out of earshot; I did some wondering about our own transport. But if they'd run off during that shooting, there was no sense hunting them before daylight. Having crawled back under the folds of the collapsed tent, we spent an uneasy night.

When along the eastern horizon a light streak began to make itself manifest, I said, "Come on. Let's get up there."

Picking up our Winchesters, hoping to sight our animals, we headed for the ridge. Being part of the eroded left-hand wall, this was no easy climb with our need to inspect all the deeper shadows and keep our eyes peeled for horses and the pair of pack mules.

We got up to the top without seeing either animals or men. "Looks like," I grumbled, "we're the last of the Mohicans."

I don't suppose he caught that allusion dragged from past reading. He was scouting around in a vain hunt for casualties. He suddenly let out a shout and, when I reached him, said, "We drew blood anyway."

There were dark stains where he pointed, and the glint of several cartridge cases. And presently we found enough empty shells to figure there'd not been more than three making all that racket. "Someone," I said, "must have taken a bad hurt; I can't think of any better reason for their leaving."

"They'll be back with help."

I nodded. "But not right away. Up till now those buggers haven't had too much to brag about. Let's go eat."

While I was heating up some sow bosom and boiled pintos, Jones went off with the shovel to ditch around the pool we'd been working. This taken care of, he came back and we ate. "What I miss most," he grinned, "is the biscuits." He helped me wash up, and then, both of us packing Winchesters, we went up to inspect the result of his trench. Eyeing this bypass, which was carrying the stream straight onto Josie's claim, I wondered why I hadn't thought of this myself. Far as the pool we'd been working was concerned it was a considerable improvement. With no fresh water coming into it and a lot that was there having leaked through my baffle, I began shoveling silt out onto the bank for Jones to swish around in his pan. Then I tore out the baffle and shoveled some more. "Gosh," he exclaimed, "them last three shovelfuls was mostly all nuggets!"

Time we took our first rest he'd filled two coffee cans with the golden pebbles. "A real bonanza," he chuckled. "How much in dollars would you reckon we've got here?"

I made a quick calculation. "In those two cans I'd guess around five thousand."

He looked at me with shining eyes. Not envious, just excited by the prospect of what we had in these pools. I was pretty excited myself. Working this stream was a stimulating business; I expect gold fever had grabbed onto both of us.

We were soon back to work. By the time we'd exhausted the present possibilities of this one pool and the shank of the afternoon was throwing long shadows, I estimated we'd taken—in those two cans and what we'd sacked—close to ten thousand dollars for this day's work.

While I was fixing two tins of corned beef for our supper, Jones said, "After tomorrow I think we better saddle up and head for town. You wouldn't want the sheriff to send Smith up here after us."

"No I wouldn't. Might be tougher to get rid of than those three we had last night." After a spell of pushing it around, I said, "In the morning we'll fill in that ditch you dug and head for home."

"What about them claim-jumpers? What if they come back an' take over this place?"

I shrugged, having no reasonable answer. "Just have to chance it, I reckon. How'd you like to be a partner in this operation?"

"Beats sheriffin'—you serious?"

"I'll talk to Josie. If she won't agree—and I'm sure she will—I'll cut you in for some of this anyway."

Our animals had come back while we'd been working and were now standing around waiting hopefully for oats. One thing you can bank on in this uncertain world: Whether it's dogs, cats or horses—and I'll include mules in that—they all know when it's time for a handout.

Twenty-Five

WE REACHED TOMBSTONE after three days of riding, just as the supper fires started sending up their smokes. In some ways I found it good to be back, but I had certainly hated abandoning Josephina's claim just when the digging was about to pay off. No telling what we'd find by the time we were able to return. We might find the stream overrun with stampeders. News of a gold strike has a quick circulation.

We'd brought back around fourteen thousand dollars' worth of nuggets, and filled our bellies at the Old Spain that evening, even staying on to watch Josephina dance. She had joined us at our table and listened wide-eyed to what we'd had to tell her.

"I think," she declared without my even mentioning it, "we should form a partnership, Alfie, you, Jones and myself. I'd no idea that claim was so valuable. If what you've brought back all came from the pool above my holding we had better stake out two more claims just to protect ourselves. How does that strike you?"

"We probably," I said, "ought to stake that stream for a whole half mile above where we were working, except we'd have no way of holding it."

"We've got to have more help. If those ruffians come back you could both be killed!"

"Well," I frowned, "that's a possibility. But who could we get that we'd be able to trust? Suppose we hire three or four men and they turn on us? We might be even worse off than we are right now."

We regarded each other in a gloomy silence. Jones, thus far, had not opened his mouth. Now he said, "Anyone we bring in on this would have to be a crack shot or he'd be no good to us. And as Alfred has already pointed out anyone we get might try to take over; we'd be spending half our time trying to keep them in line."

We were certainly between a rock and a hard place.

"Better sleep on it," I said. "Maybe something will turn up."

Josephina, looking worried, said, "If that sort of thing is going to continue I don't want you risking your lives up there." Then she said angrily, "Can't the law do anything to stop those ruffians?"

"Different jurisdiction. We'd be forced to deal with the sheriff of that county. We don't know anything about him," I said.

And Jones remarked, "Most sheriffs nowadays are politicians, inclined to consider votes when interpreting the law. If we hired a big enough well-armed crew I doubt if that bunch would bother us. But . . . I feel like Alfie—how could we trust them?"

Josephina said, "Do you truly think, Alfie, there's enough gold there to be worth such a risk."

"It's there all right. I'm going back anyway whatever we decide. It's my opinion it's worth hanging onto."

"Who's the biggest cowman in that neck of the woods?" Jones asked.

"Armagón Posada," Josie said. "He controls a great deal of that county."

"Would he let us have enough men to work five claims?"

"A lot of his relations are living off him," she said. "I imagine he'd be happy to be rid of a few."

"Without being cut in?" I asked, skeptically.

"He has no interest in mines," Josie said. "All he thinks about is cows. But if he understands what you're up against I think he might let you have four or five men we could put some dependence on—nobody's anxious to cross up Posada. He can influence a lot of votes in that country."

"Do you know him?" I asked.

She shrugged. "We are acquainted. A little bit."

"Could you talk to him?"

I thought she looked a little dubious, but she said, "I can try."

"Well," I said, pushing back my chair, "we better see Behan and find out where we're at."

Behan said, "I'm glad you're back in time to be of some use. Judge has decided to put on the case of the people versus our four prisoners at ten o'clock tomorrow morning."

"How much time will this kill?"

"If I know the judge it will take no longer than he can help."

"Prosecutor think he can get a conviction?"

"He's coming up for re-election," Behan remarked significantly.

"And he'll be trying Dry Camp along with those other three?"

"That's his intention. They're certainly connected.

Once the court hears your testimony I don't see how Dry Camp will be able to wriggle clear; and Fred Hume's here to represent Wells-Fargo."

"Can you keep Josephina out of this?"

He shook his head. "She's a material witness. She'll be summoned."

The trial went off like clockwork. In two days of hearings the four men were convicted, and Jones—who'd quit his deputy's job—set off with me for that talk with Armagón Posada. I carried a note for him from Josie— "On account of my mother it might have a little weight," she said. "Don Armagón is old-fashioned, thinks a woman's place is in the home."

Three days later we were sitting with Don Armagón in the attractive *sala* of his ranch house being refreshed with little cakes and wine. "A rare vintage," I said, and the old man nodded complacently.

"I import it from Spain. Now perhaps you will say how I can be of service."

So I told him of our partnership with Josephina and handed him her letter, which—excusing himself—he read with no change of expression. I told him of her restaurant and the fine Spanish meals she served, including Spanish music and one flamenco dance each evening. "As you may know, she owns a small claim some ten miles from here. More capital was needed. She asked me to have a look at her claim and, if feasible, work it, hoping we could bring back enough gold to allow all the things she has it in mind to do for the place."

The old man nodded. "She must have a lot of faith in the integrity of you gentlemen." He regarded us thoughtfully. "And what did you find?"

"It is our present intention to stake out four more claims," I said. "We are not alone in believing she has a bonanza there. I've turned back two lots of would-be claim-jumpers. We've reason to think they'll be back with additional ruffians. Our problem is to get together a trustworthy crew to defend this ground."

Posada gravely nodded once more. "Quite so."

"Yes, well . . . she thought perhaps you might help us."

Don Armagón smiled. "In what fashion?"

"She thought you might furnish several trustworthy men."

He thought about that. "How many would you require?"

"We have thought that perhaps four would be sufficient, allowing each man to share equally with us in the four new claims we're planning to stake. After doing a bit of prospecting it's my belief the five claims will provide for the restaurant and a very good living for the men we need."

"You say you've looked this ground over. How far upstream would four additional claims take you?"

"Something more than a quarter mile. These nuggets are coming down from somewhere farther up the canyon."

"But if someone staked above you, mightn't he cut off the flow?"

"Only if we were unable to prevent it," I told him grimly, and I thought his look held a little more approval.

"I believe," he said, "you should stake enough claims to blanket the first half mile. With six determined shareholders I would imagine you might control that much." He looked again at the youthful Jones.

"Jones," I said, "has been working with me and can verify what I've told you."

The old man smiled at the optimism of youth. "If I were ten years younger I'd go up there with you. If you'd care to stay over and honor my poor home I think by tomorrow I shall have an answer."

At around ten the next morning we were summoned to the *sala*. Six sombreroed men stood about the room. Don Armagón invited us to take chairs beside him. "These fellows are relations of mine, young, impetuous, with an eye for adventure. I think you will find them adequate." One or two, darker than the others, showed, I thought, a bit of Indian blood. All in all a competent-looking group. "Tell them your proposition," Posada said. "They are free to go or decline, as they choose."

So I went over it again, holding nothing back. While their eyes were questioning each other, the old man said, "I have a suggestion. I believe if you and they were to form a mining company you would all be in a much stronger position."

"Makes sense," I said. "I'll mention this to Josephina." And to the others I said, "What is your feeling? Does this interest you?"

They appeared to be unanimously for it.

"I take it you have weapons?"

"On the *caballos*," the tallest man said.

"I have a paper here that will require your signatures." I handed it to Posada, who read it and nodded. "Sign," he told them.

When they had done so and the paper was back in my pocket, I thanked Don Armagón for his help and hospitality. To the men, now our partners, I said, "We've got a thirty-mile ride ahead of us. I think we should be on our way."

No one had asked where this claim was located, and to me this seemed a bit on the queer side . . . unless they already knew.

Twenty-Six

WITH A SIGNED blank check Josie had given me, we waited on the outskirts of Broken Butte while Jones rode in to buy the supplies and tools we were going to need, and additional mules to transport these. I'd have really preferred to have outfitted in Tombstone or Benson, but with no idea how many to buy for, that had not appeared very practical.

I had already asked if any of our new partners had placer mining experience; it seemed two of them had done some prospecting and panning: Chico Valdez, a gregarious chap with steel-rimmed spectacles, and Eladio Guerero, a big burly cove who looked strong enough to tie bar iron into a knot. He had a knife scar on one cheek and a limp he claimed to have acquired playing "bezball."

While we were awaiting the return of Jones, I suggested the need of establishing a pecking system. "I shall represent the *patrona* with Señor Jones for an assistant, a kind of straw boss. Guerero will represent the new partners. Is this acceptable?"

Assured that it was, I said, "All of us are free to stake out a private claim, and should the *patrona* decide to form a mining company all such claims, including hers, will become company property, each of us having an equal interest except that half the original claim shall be hers absolutely. Is this agreeable?"

No one objecting, I assumed that it was. One thing continued to be a burr in my bonnet. Why had Posada been so extremely obliging? What did he expect to get out of it? From all I had heard the man was far from altruistically inclined. With so much good fortune appearing to ride in our direction, why was I feeling so mistrustful?

I said to Jones when he returned with his purchases, including oats, packed aboard three stout mules, "Reckon you're up to getting back to Josephina with a report on the Posada visit, the six new partners and the old man's suggestion about forming a company? I'd like you also to inquire about the sluice I asked Josie to order. If she favors forming a company ask if she'll have the papers drawn up, allowing you to return with a copy for each partner."

"Gotcha." Jones nodded and set off straightaway.

When we reached the site of our endeavors, apparently all was just as we had left it. No sign of intruders that I was able to find. I explained the procedure for staking out claims. "You'd better get at this at once," I said, after pointing out Josephina's ground. "When this has been done come back and we'll eat."

First thing next morning I went over the need of keeping an eye skinned for strangers. "You should realize these persons are determined to drive us away from here. Once you've staked you've a bona fide right to protect your property."

Three of our new partners I placed in strategic positions to keep track of our animals and watch for intruders. I put the others to digging a new diversion trench around one side of each pool to facilitate the recovery of nuggets. "Keep your rifles close at hand."

I was not expecting trouble this soon but thought it well to be prepared.

On the following day I took over the duty of watching for intruders and put the rest of them to work sifting the silt and gravel of their claims. These efforts, with each of the partners handling his own food requirements, produced about fifteen hundred dollars' worth of gold for a first day's work.

It occurred to me that evening that each of us would have to write out a legal description of the claims we'd staked and that someone would have to be sent with these to the county seat for recording. Because the man appeared less interested in work than the rest of our outfit, I gave Chico Valdez the privilege of making sure these claims were properly recorded.

After he'd set off with the location notices, I arranged with the others that three shots fired close together would bring everyone on the run. A kind of uneasiness or vague disquiet had begun to rub at my nerve ends, and search as I would, I could discover no adequate reason for this. Everything appeared to be going well.

Next day, still with myself doing sentinel duty, I gave one of the partners the responsibility of keeping an eye on our remuda. Chico Valdez was back the next morning from his trip to the county seat.

With the claims now properly recorded I felt easier in mind. On the following evening Frisco Jones was back from Tombstone with word from Josephina. "First off," he reported, "she didn't much like that 'company' notion, but when I told her you were all for it she said we would go ahead with it."

He produced a batch of official-looking papers from inside his vest. "These," he said, handing them to me, "are the partnership papers, one for each of the six new men, one for you and one for me, all properly inscribed and signed by Josephina."

"That last clause," I mentioned, "prohibiting any partner from selling or assigning his recorded claim to any outsider without the expressed and written permission of the president of the company—Josephina herself—could prove a pretty smart addition, protecting all of us."

Passed out and read, this partnership agreement produced no objections. Which, in a way, I couldn't help but find surprising. A very agreeable bunch, I was reflecting when Chico Valdez spoke up to say he was not interested in belonging to a company and would keep his claim for himself as sole owner. This occasioned considerable astonishment on the part of his companions. "Why," I asked, "have you made this decision after the partnership papers—?"

"Well," he broke in, "I like to be my own man, do what I please and whenever I feel like. I'm not a peon to be ordered about. If I want to go elsewhere I don't want a fool paper holding me here."

"Why didn't you say this while we were still at the ranch and this was discussed?"

"The old man wouldn't have liked it and I wanted to have a look at this setup."

"And now that you're here you don't care to be a part of it?"

He showed a saturnine grin. "That's about the size of it."

I didn't like this. His friends didn't either. One man spoke up to say, "If he refuses to join the company and abide by its rules he should not be allowed a claim."

Several others nodded, eyeing Valdez in a hostile manner.

Deciding anything I might say at this time would
only aggravate the matter and perhaps create some further resentment, I showed them a smile and beckoned
Jones aside. "Did you learn anything of that sluice I
ordered?"

"Yep. It's on its way. Being freighted. I passed the
teams about twenty miles back. What's your notion about
this Chico hombre? Think he's out to make trouble?"

"I'm doing some wondering about him. I think he's
been got at. Better keep an eye on him."

"You reckon he could be furtherin' some scheme of
Posada's?"

I managed a shrug. "We'll have to watch him."

That evening I had a few words with this misfit.
"What's eating you, Chico?"

"Not a thing," he said, grinning.

I wished I could see the eyes back of his spectacles. "If
you don't like it here you don't have to stay, you know."

"I like it fine."

"You found no fault with this program when Don
Armagón suggested it."

"You don't find fault with Posada's notions."

"All right," I said. "Good luck with your claim." There
wasn't any sense getting steamed up about it. I watched
him go tramping off toward his claim, which was farther
up the canyon, last of the line, well upstream from
Josephina's holding, which was marked Number One
on the company map.

I got hold of Guerero. "What's the matter with Chico?"

Our crew boss shrugged. "A hard man to know—what
you call a 'loner.' The patron, I'm think, was glad to be
rid of him."

"You reckon, now he's outside the company, he'll do the work he agreed to when we allowed him to stake that claim?"

"He might. *Quien sabe?*"

A fine kettle of fish, I thought to myself. To have this fellow right here in our bosom, and with no allegiance to the rest of us, was the kind of thing I had hoped to avoid when promoting Posada's suggestion. "Keep an eye on him," I said, and, picking up a shovel, joined the others who were putting in the diversion ditches.

First off I'd thought, when I met the man at Posada's, those steel-rimmed specs gave him a studious look, a sort of scholarly connotation. Now I was not sure what they did for him other than make his intentions unreadable. I had a hunch I ought to light a fire under him and am not sure yet why I didn't. I expect it was probably in the hope of not alienating anyone else. We were sitting on a powder keg here. I didn't want any matches thrown round.

For the rest of the day Chico kept to himself, fooling round on his claim or squatting there with his back against a rock making doodles in the dust. Far as I was able to see he didn't put in one lick of work. I had the disquieting notion he was waiting for something.

Guerero seemed to pick up my thought, because a couple hours later he dropped by to say, "I'm watching that hombre. I'll see that he don't kick up any squabbles."

But the fun had gone clean out of the day. I'd been worried enough by thoughts of those blackguards who had shot up our camp when Jones and myself were the only ones here. Keeping a watch out for them and having this loose fish right in our midst was enough to make damn near anyone curse.

Only four hundred nuggets were picked up that day, but this was because of all the digging we'd done. The gold was here, I'd no doubt about that. Tomorrow I'd turn Jones loose on our claim with a couple of the partners to help him. It crossed my mind that as more and more nuggets were dug out of the creek, some central cache would have to be found for them, and I wondered if this was what Chico was waiting for. I put it up to Guerero. "You reckon he'll try to make off with them?"

"Be pretty reckless. A couple of those boys would think nothing of killing him if he was to be caught trying anything like that."

Sometime that night Valdez saddled up and rode off without a word to anyone.

Watching the partners digging into that muck, I found it hard to picture Josie up to her thighs in this gurgling stream. But when she'd walked into the Russ House that day and dumped those nuggets on the counter in front of me, she hadn't been dressed in her current fashion. I remembered the flash of dark eyes and that grin. The mercurial person she'd been in those days was hard to equate with the girl she'd become since we'd opened that restaurant, the businesswoman Jones and I had talked with before coming up here. Not many laughs in her these days.

Nor in me, I thought grimly.

A couple hours after sunup the sheriff arrived with a warrant for my arrest.

Twenty-Seven

HE DID NOT announce this straightaway.

The guard on the ridge wigwagged to tell us someone was approaching the bend in the canyon. I'd been talking with Jones as we rested on our shovels, and both of us, sober-faced, let go of these to pick up our rifles. A few minutes later we saw him, a heavy-set man in cowpuncher rig beneath a dusty black Stetson, on a zebra-striped dun, with a six-shooter dangling from his belt at either hip. We watched him taking a good look around before pulling up a few feet away from us. He said, "Which of you fellers is Addlington?"

"I am," I said. "What's on your mind?"

He rasped a blunt-fingered hand along the side of his jaw, being careful not to disturb his handlebar mustache. "Surprised to find so many of you working this claim."

"How's that?"

"Well, it's like this. I was told you were out here with just one helper."

"Who sold you that notion?"

"Darcy LaRue—man who owns this claim."

"Don't know him. What's he look like?"

The description he gave matched the claim-jumper I'd run off after shooting his partner. I said as much.

The man nodded. "He told me you'd probably take that line." He pulled open his coat to show the badge on his vest.

"This claim," Jones said, "belongs to Josephina who owns the Old Spain restaurant in Tombstone."

The sheriff chucked him a frosty glance. "I took the trouble to have a look at the book before I rode down here. This claim is recorded in the name of Darcy LaRue."

His glance swung to me. "I have a warrant for your arrest. You are charged with killing his employee, Buck Baldwin, and running LaRue off his claim at gunpoint."

I said, "He may have told you that, but I was sent here to work this claim for Josephina. She said I'd find her location notice. What I found was two claim-jumpers helping themselves to some of her gold. This Baldwin pulled a gun on me and I shot him. The other one, this LaRue, I suppose, dug for the tullies."

"You can tell that to the court when you come up for trial. LaRue deposes furthermore that when he returned a couple weeks later with two of his friends you had another feller with you—him," he said, pointing at Jones, "and that the pair of you opened fire on them, grievously wounding one of his companions with a Sharps rifle. LaRue states further that, having nothing but six-shooters and this badly wounded friend, they were forced to leave you in possession in order to get him to a doctor. The wounded man died on the way. I'm going to have to take you in," he declared, ignoring the threat of Jones's lifted rifle.

"A bunch of damn lies from start to finish!" Jones growled.

"I expect," the sheriff said mildly, "the court will be able to sift out the truth. One thing's for sure: the courthouse records at the patent office show Darcy LaRue as the legal owner of this claim. Get your horse, Addlington."

"Look," I said, "the lady who really owns this claim has formed a company and these people you see are all partners—"

"I know my duty. Are you coming peaceably—"

"The charge is preposterous. Of course I'm not coming."

The lawman swept a look about and nodded. "Very well. I shall be back with a posse," he declared with a darkening face. "You are only making it hard on yourself, resisting an officer in performance of his duty."

He wheeled his horse and departed.

Everyone it seemed like after his departure started talking at once. "They can't get away with this," Jones said, looking worried. "Can they?"

"They seem to think they can. Somebody, obviously, has tampered with the records. Perhaps I should have gone with him. Thrashed this out in court."

"I don't think you would ever have gotten there. The Mexicans have a phrase for it. Killed while attempting to escape." He shook his head. "By God, we're not going to let them cut that kind of rusty!"

"I don't want you fellows laying up trouble for yourselves."

Jones snorted. Guerero said through his chaw of tobacco, "I think now we'll find Chico never recorded our claims. Whoever is back of this is counting on grabbing the whole stream."

"We can stand them off," Jones cried, excited.

I said, "Maybe he's bluffing," but I didn't believe it. He'd be back all right. Having gone this far, he had to be fixing to go all the way.

The bare-faced gall of it made my blood boil.

Twenty-Eight

THE PARTNERS, WHO'D come running at the first sign of trouble, looked stunned at the sheriff's outrageous accusations. I could see how neatly I'd been framed. Very neatly, indeed.

Real anger distorted Guerero's face as he caught hold of my arm. "I will go to Don Armagón, señor. He has influence—friends in high places. I will tell him of this thing."

"Later," I said, trying to see some way out.

Another man said, "But the county attorney—the *abogado,* owes much to the Posadas! Surely, he—"

"One of you," I said, "should go to the recorder's office and look at the book." But I felt, even then, they would discover Darcy LaRue listed as legal owner of Josephina's claim. I could not see or account for the sheriff's confident assurance in any other way.

Guerero declared, "I shall go at once, *amigo*. I will take the extra horse to get there soonest."

Clamoring notions clattered through my head like a stampede of cattle, none of these making enough sense to grab onto. I felt like a fly caught up in a spider's web. This bad thing that had latched onto me showed all the hallmarks of a plan set up with devilish care; but as time dragged on and the shadows lengthened, I was clutched by a reckless fury at the chain of frustrations that, it seemed, had maneuvered me into this impossible situation.

It was hard to focus on what I *could* do. Not much, this was evident. I might run, for whatever that might be worth, or I could face them with violence until their sheer weight in numbers pulled me down.

Running would get me nowhere; it could only enlarge their contention of guilt.

If I stayed and fought, one man against all of them, there was the barest chance I might create enough havoc—as had happened with that gun feud at Lincoln— that some rumor of the uproar might carry beyond the sheriff's jurisdiction. A hare-brained thought, but the way I finally chose to go.

I scouted the slopes for places of concealment, for positions from which I could inflict the most damage. By the time my companions sat down to supper, I'd pretty well mapped out the course I would take. I had plenty of Winchester cartridges. I'd not fire first—let them bear the onus of that. I'd learned enough about posses to be sure some skylarking fool would turn loose his artillery regardless of what that sheriff might order.

I slept very little, awakened in the blackness by a hand roughly shaking me, and Guerero's voice. "Our number one claim is recorded at the top of a page in the name of LaRue. But there are numbers missing—the page just ahead had been cut from the book. I looked more than once before discovering this. What shall we do?"

"Stay out of this. All of you."

I caught the flash of white teeth. "Too late for that. None of our claims are in that book. We have taken a vote—all five of us. We will do what you do."

"They'll not come for a prisoner. Someone out there wants me out of the picture."

"But, señor—"

"Stay out of this, Guerero! They want me dead. Tell your friends to get out of this canyon—"

"They will not go."

"If they stay and that sheriff can contrive it you will all be killed—don't you understand? They can't afford to leave witnesses!"

"We will see about that. I'm thinking you better get up."

Already the sky was beginning to lighten. I'd left Singlefoot picketed just outside the tent and had only to slosh on my hat, step into my boots and pick up my rifle. I was ready as I ever would be.

All the partners were up. I guessed most of them had eaten. All had rifles and looked ready to use them. "You get the hell out of here!" I told Jones, and he laughed.

Guerero said, "I have saddled your mare."

I nodded, shoved a boot in the stirrup and swung aboard. I swept a look across those determined faces. They'd no intention of leaving unless I did. "You're a good bunch, boys. I'm proud to have known you." Jones got into his saddle; there were no other horses in sight. I turned the mare, pointing her nose at the far slope's rim, Jones right behind me.

That sheriff must have been an anxious man. Scarcely had we reached the rim, topping out, than Jones called, "They're here!"

Twisting my head for a backward look, I saw a dark huddle of horsemen tear round the bend, aiming straight for our claims, rifles a-glint in the brightening light as they converged on the camp. Then, as I'd expected, some overeager fool couldn't wait and ripped off a shot. One of our partners was down, the rest diving for cover when Jones started firing. The horsebackers broke apart in a hurry, the flat crack of a Winchester sweeping Jones from the saddle. I couldn't know that he was dead, but he certainly looked it, lying all spraddled out.

There must have been ten or twelve men in that posse; seemed plain, one way or another, they meant to carry me off this time. Down below there was a confusion of rearing, screaming, pitching horses, guns going off all over the place as men scattered for cover, a pair of riderless mounts pelting hellity-larrup back toward the bend they had just come round.

Once they were out of sight, I flung off the mare in a flying leap, scurrying back toward the brush-lined edge where, at least partially concealed, I could look down on the battle raging below. The possemen—those still able—were off their horses and down behind boulders, returning the partners' fire, obviously intent on leaving no survivors.

Only three rifles were now returning the invaders' shots. From where I bellied up to the rim, I could see the sprawled shapes of three of the sheriff's outfit who wouldn't be bothering anyone for supper. I could pick out the sheriff in his ten-gallon hat where he crouched behind a lopsided rock, not exposing himself to do any shooting. I took a bead on his hat and knocked it off, but he had squirmed around now to where I couldn't see him.

Three of the posse had stayed in their saddles till they'd got out of range; now, dismounted, they were endeavoring to outflank our boys, wriggling along from cover to cover. Taking careful aim, remembering I was shooting downhill and trying to allow for this, I squeezed off a shot at the one in the lead, saw him jerk and twist over.

Turning my attention to the fellow behind him, I fired again and missed him completely, as attested by his hurry to find a new refuge. I was able, however, to drop the man back of him.

During a lull in the firing two more of the posse were sneaking nearer the three surviving partners, one of whom looked like Guerero. It was one of this pair who reopened the fight. I backed off a ways, found a new vantage and sent one of these two up into plain view with a leg shot, and one of our boys knocked him over. It was now that I finally discovered LaRue.

Like the sheriff, he'd been staying well back of the others. It was a ricochet that scared him into my sights. I fired and saw him jerk and lurch sideways, try to get back under cover, jerk again and collapse like a pricked balloon.

I looked back for Jones and presently discovered he had done no moving since being swept from his saddle. I had to reckon he was dead; they had certainly wanted to make sure of him, the only witness I had to the previous gunplay. I then discovered to my surprise that the sheriff and three of the posse still able to move had got onto the three horses left back out of range, two of them riding double as they disappeared behind the bend in the canyon that cut off our view.

Guerero called up to me. *"Que pasar?"*

"They've quit, what's left of them—pulling out.

When, aboard Singlefoot, I got back down to the stream, I found that of our partners, Guerero and one other were the only ones unscathed. Of the other three, two were dead and the third badly wounded. We patched him up as best we could. Guerero and the other survivor went hunting for horses and presently came back mounted, leading one of our mules.

When we had got the wounded man onto the mule, Guerero said, "I've got to get Pepe to a doctor," and I nodded. He said, "You better come with us. That sheriff will be back."

"Probably," I agreed, and saw Guerero studying me.

"You stay here you'll be a sitting duck."

"They've got me boxed no matter what I do. LaRue is dead. I just had a look at him. We've killed at least seven of that posse—maybe eight. They'll not forget it. If you can find some way to make Chico Valdez and that recorder talk it may change the picture. Otherwise we're outlaws—fair game for anyone packing a badge."

"I'll see Don Armagón," Guerero said. I remembered he had said this before.

Twenty-Nine

IT TOOK ME a good while to bury the dead. The afternoon was well advanced when the freighter and his swamper arrived with our sluice and helped me assemble it in a level stretch of the creek. I had no hope of ever getting to use it. With so many dead there'd be no getting out of this; all I could do to offset this frame was to make it as costly as possible for whatever persons the framers sent after me.

The sheriff, I figured, just about had to be in on this. Something about him when he'd arrived with that warrant had convinced me.

The freighter had seemed astonished to find no other fellows working the claims, so I gave him a short summary of the day's events. I also put into his keeping all the nuggets we had gathered and asked him to see that Josephina got them. I gave him our version of the fight, which I'd written out for the *Tombstone Epitaph*, and asked if he'd take it to Clum, the paper's owner, which he said he would.

He said, "Weren't you one of Behan's deputies?"

"For a while."

I cooked up a batch of refried beans, which they shared before leaving. "If it's like you say," declared the freighter earnestly, "I don't guess you oughta hang around this place."

"You're probably right," I admitted, "but where would I go?"

"Come back with us. Get outa this county. Why play into their hands?"

"I'm in so far now there don't seem much point in running. No problem to track me down. This claim belongs to Josie. I'll stay and rattle for long as I'm able."

Watching them drive off, I bent and picked up my rifle. Went inside the tent and dumped a measure of oats in the nosebag for Singlefoot and stood around with my thoughts till she'd emptied it. I'd been meaning to turn her loose to go find the rest of our stock and be out of the way of the next batch of fireworks; but I left the saddle on her and slipped the bit back into her mouth before putting the nosebag where I'd been keeping it.

There wasn't much left to do that I could see but make it as costly as possible for the law and whoever it was serving, confident they'd be back with more help; the sheriff could no longer afford to have me get away from him. Whatever talk of this swindle got afoot on account of this shoot-out he would want to come from his side of the fence.

Mostly I'd figured to stay and do what I could to hold Josie's claim; since I was bound to die anyway, to have it chalked up to defending her interests. Might help in the long run to legitimize her right to it. Another reason I hadn't aimed to run was the conviction that when he returned the sheriff would be fetching a Navajo tracker. It didn't seem likely he'd be expecting me to wait for him.

To let his readers have a truthful account of what had gone on here was why I'd written it down for that freighter to fetch back to Clum at the *Tombstone Epitaph*. But during another spell of cogitation I cleaned and reloaded my Winchester—something I'd almost forgotten to do—and had second thoughts about being a sitting duck for those buggers. I turned the mare Bill Brady had got for me at Lincoln toward the shelving slope of the canyon's far wall, mostly to make sure there was nobody up there.

And I was thinking of Josie, deciding I wanted to see her again, remembering how she'd come after me at Galeyville, getting me out of that ice house trap, possibly saving my life. Looking over the pictures of her lodged in my mind. And discovering before much more time had passed how it might have been better had I stuck to my original intention and cashed in my chips at the claim.

If a man could look ahead of his impulsive actions— have at least some idea of where they'd be taking him— a good many things would probably never get done.

Despair for the things that might have been was riding me hard as I came onto the ridge where LaRue and his understrapper had fired down into our camp that night. A wildness was again boiling up through my thinking. All the things I'd been up against since quitting that train at Albuquerque began to prod at my temper as we picked our way through the piñon brush when I ought to've been keeping my eyes skinned for trouble.

First thing I knew we'd come into a clearing and there in the moonglow half a rope's length away sat two grinning riders behind leveled rifles.

I guess I must have gone crazy. Never had I been so quick in my life to get the gun off my hip and squeeze trigger. The nearest rider went off his rearing horse backward. The second one didn't even attempt to shoot back but flung himself flat along the neck of his bolting pony and went crashing away through the second-growth pines without being hit by the slugs I threw after him. I probably should have given chase instead of wheeling my mare to go larruping off in another direction, but thinking hadn't caught up with me yet. All I wanted right then was to get clean off of that ridge in a hurry.

I did, too. Ducking tree limbs, hurdling rocks, we struck off south at a pace I can only recall as plumb reckless. Time I got hold of myself I'd no idea where I'd got to except it must have been at least a couple miles from that ridge.

There must have been more than I'd thought in that posse. Thinking to make sure of me, I reckoned, the sheriff had split up his outfit, and this pair I had met hadn't been in that ruckus, had been sent prowling the pines to take care of any partners who managed to get clear. Like a fool, I'd run into them.

Looked like my best bet now was to strike out for Tombstone—at least get out of that rascal's jurisdiction. I wasn't sure where I was, so I kept heading south.

As I jogged along with this intention, a good many notions jumped around through my head, none of them helpful. The pines were behind me. I was coming down into foothills with sprangles of greasewood, an occasional yucca. Much as possible I skirted the hilltops, clung to the arroyos, hoping to keep out of sight. These did not always go the way I wanted, but after that last confrontation I was leery of being picked up by a glass.

It seemed to me now that if I could reach Tombstone I'd at least have some kind of chance to stay healthy.

Coming out of the brushy ravine I'd just traveled, a strong instinct to stop laid hold of me. And I did, waiting stiffly, nothing tangible in sight. Still I sat, scarce breathing, eyes darting about in the bleak hunt for danger. The mare's ears were pricked, listening, the rifle across my pommel feeling sweaty in my clutch.

Then I caught the faint sound of nearing hoofs, and in a blind panic I spun Singlefoot round and took off up my backtrail. I'd seen a draw back a ways, a sort of side canyon, which I hoped to get into before I could be spotted. There, I pulled up behind a jumble of boulders, where I slid from the saddle to wait crouched with my Winchester ready for action. And heard them go past—two or three by the sound.

But just as I was fixing to take off again, the hoof sound stopped and then resumed more slowly after a moment. I guessed one of them anyway was coming back for a look. I was loath to go farther into this gorge, afraid there might be no other way out.

For several minutes nothing happened. The hoof sound had quit. I thought possibly the rider had got off his horse, and I happened just then to swivel a look at the crumbly wall above me. I caught a blur of motion, sent a slug up there and piled into leather, driving the mare back into the ravine. I saw the man on foot and fired just as he did, not waiting to see if I'd scored or not.

Another bad mistake.

I never even heard the shot that dropped me.

When I recovered consciousness—came back to a realization of my surroundings—I was no longer out in the hills and gullies but penned up securely in a six-by-eight cell with a single barred window, a bed and slop bucket, and a faraway glimpse of the hills off yonder.

Thirty

IN THE FOUR months of my captivity I hadn't once seen Josephina. In a way that was the hardest to bear. The rifle shot that had put me here had healed long since. I was fed twice a day but never taken from this second-floor room. The only thing outside I was able to look at were blue mountains and, eventually, the top of a gallows.

I had about given up all hope of a reprieve when Guerero came in the third week to see me. We eyed each other for some while without speaking. "What happened to the two partners you went off with? Did that wounded fellow die?"

"No, señor. He is walking some now, not far of course. The others are all right. They are working again at the ranch."

"And Josephina?"

"She cooks in her restaurant. There has been much discussion of you in the papers. I would have fetched them, amigo, had this been allowed."

"Do you know when I'll be tried?"

He considered me some more. Finally he said, "You were tried right after they brought you here."

I didn't remember, not that it made any difference. The result of any trial was a foregone conclusion. Men had died; I had killed some of them. They don't erect gallows without they figure to use them. "When will I be hanged?"

Guerero shrugged. *"Quien sabe?"*

"Good-bye, old friend," I said, squeezing his hand, and called for the guard.

He came twice more. He had talked several times, he said, with Don Armagón. Answering the old man's questions, he'd gone over the whole thing—as much as he'd known—several times. The *patron* had also questioned the other surviving partners, but got little from them.

I had thought, when first I'd realized where I was, that I was done for, that I could have died better defending the claim.

The last time Guerero came, about a week ago, he seemed pretty excited. "The *patrona* has visited Don Armagón! I do not know what was said. They talked a long while. In the papers they are calling you the sheriff killer. Only the *Epitaph* has a good word for you."

I could not remember killing the sheriff, though I did recall knocking his hat off.

"Señor Clum's paper has been calling for your release; they have printed several times the story you sent in by the freighter. They are calling you the victim of a 'dastardly plot.' They keep saying the claim belongs to Josephina, that LaRue and those others were claim-jumpers."

I had thought I had become resigned to my fate, but found that hope dies hard. No matter how unreasonable it may seem, half-hidden away at the back of one's mind one continues to believe that something will come up in the end to save one. Over and over like a horse on a treadmill I'd reviewed the happenings that had led up to my being here, and was doing so again when I realized Guerero was still speaking. "Chico has been arrested and Don Armagón has twice talked with the governor.

Maybe we get you out of here yet."

But the gallows was ready and waiting for me to be marched up the steps. You could not get around that.

After Guerero left I went over what he'd told me. This was the second week into the fourth month I had been here. Surely the people's case against me must have run into a snag or they'd have hanged me already. Even if they'd got a confession from Valdez about his part in this chain of events, I could not see how that could much help me. I reckoned the only way I could get off was if somehow it could be proved our number one claim— Josephina's—legally belonged to her. And even this, I thought, might not be sufficient to exonerate me with so many dead men laid at my door.

Time dragged like a man with a gimpy leg.

On the last day of the fourth month of my stay in this place I had a visit from the under sheriff, a tall, shambling man with a walrus mustache. "Just stopped by to say your time's about up, Addlington. I'll leave you to wonder how it will feel to have a rope around your neck. Tomorrow's the big day. We've sold enough tickets to pack that yard. We'll get the show on the road at four o'clock."

I bade hope good-bye. In a way I'd be glad to get it over and done with.

They were not the best prospects in the world to go to bed with. I spent an uneasy night but managed by dint of considerable effort to get outside the big first-class breakfast that came my way at eight the next morning. I supposed there'd be a lot of reporters; none had ever been allowed in to see me. In all this time the only visitor I'd had, and him not often, was Eladio Guerero.

They sent a barber up to shave me and an hour or so later allowed a sky pilot in, case I cared to make my peace with God. "I've done nothing to be shrived for," I told him. "What I did was done in good faith to protect our property and this life they're about to take."

After his departure, having delivered himself of several platitudes, I stared out through the bars on my window past the top of the scaffold to the shapes of blue mountains I could see in the distance.

By two o'clock I was pacing the floor, stopping now and again to peer out at the mountains, wishing I was in them and wondering why Josie hadn't ever come to see me. She'd been busy, of course, with the restaurant and all, but still . . .

I blew out a sigh and resumed my pacing.

At a little after three a guard came with a key and unlocked my door. "You're wanted downstairs. Get a move on."

When I stepped into the warden's office the first thing I heard was "Oh, Alfie!" and there was Josephina flinging her arms around my neck and snuggling a wet cheek against my own.

"Don't cry," I said gruffly. "We've all of us got to die sometime. Tell me, how have you been? How are things at the restaurant? Will you be able to make it without that claim?"

She stepped back and the better to see me wiped her eyes on the back of a hand.

"You're free—didn't they tell you? The governor has pardoned you!"

I stared at her stupidly, unable to believe. "Free? Governor? What did he want to do that for?"

"They should have told you," she cried. "I have your

release right here in my hand!" She shook me. "Close your mouth, Alfie—you look like a bird waiting to be fed. Here! Read it for yourself! A complete exoneration!"

I had a hard time taking it in. I would have liked to sit down but didn't reckon I'd better. I felt like if I moved I would fall plumb apart.

I gave the paper back to her. "But the governor . . ." I began.

She said, "I talked to him myself. Posada talked to him—Johnny Behan did too, and told the new sheriff up there he would vouch for you, said you were an honest man, the best deputy he ever had! They've set that bogus trial aside. The county recorder finally confessed his part in the conspiracy, produced the missing page, admitted the claim was legally mine, and Guerero had recorded, just yesterday, the claims of our company partners. Oh, I've so much to tell you I hardly know where to begin!"

And here I thought she'd forgotten me.

Seeing her, hearing her, certainly went a long way toward shaking me loose of the notions I'd been living with. And "Oh, yes," she said, "two of those surviving deputies have also been arrested . . ."

She stamped her foot. "What's the matter with you?— Aren't you *glad*?"

"I . . . Yes . . . I guess so—I'll be glad to get out of here, certainly. That sheriff—"

"Has been charged with being one of the ringleaders. He was LaRue's uncle—can you beat that! Chico, when the governor started looking into this, broke down and admitted his part in the affair; it was that recorder himself who cut the page from the records—oh, come *on*, let's get out of here!"

I had no strenuous objection to that. Tugging me

along, she said in that take-charge way she had, "It's time we did some talking about *us!*" and I wasn't too adamantly set against that.

And there at the outside gate was my Singlefoot mare I'd been counting as lost, shaking her head and whinnying, pawing at the ground, softly blowing through her nostrils as we came nearer, those dark eyes filled with pleasure and excitement. I could see she hadn't forgotten me.

Josephina, sounding exasperated, said, "You're not listening to a thing I say!"

"Well . . . I heard some of it. Guerero said Posada had been to see the governor twice about me. Why should a man important as Don Armagón put himself to such a bother for a landless gringo already in his debt and, moreover, a chap he hadn't seen but once in his life?"

"Don't stare at me that way!" she said, coloring up the way she had when I'd first known her. "Why shouldn't he exert himself a little?" And there was that toplofty look I remembered. "I told you way back he was a kind of connection . . ."

"Don't take that line with me, my girl! I've a right, by grab, to know what I've got into. Stop evading the question."

"Why shouldn't he put himself out for me? My own mother's brother—"

"Indeed," I said. "And where does the cow and the bull come in, *vaca y toro?*"

She blushed again. "That part I made up. You were being such a ninny! I thought that big oaf El Miga had turned you off the Posadas . . ."

"Yes, but I still—"

"I told him you were . . ."

"Let's have the whole truth for a change," I said, eyeing her. "It couldn't be you told him I was busting to marry you. I can't see that building such a fire under him."

"Why you scowl, hombre? You have no longer the wish to marry weeth me?"

"Just answer the question! How did you persuade him? Did you tell him," I said, "you couldn't live without me?"

"You're a stinker!" she cried, stamping her foot again, cheeks all afire. Stamped it again. Then, despite her vexation, her eyes flashed with laughter. "Of course I did. The second time I went up there I said I was expecting . . ."

"You never!"

"Yes I did! How else could I have moved him? If you back out on me now he's apt to do you a mischief—"

"Hell, I wouldn't back out for all the nuggets in that stream!" I said, and found myself abruptly locked in her arms. I like to never caught my breath.

Nelson Nye was born in Chicago, Illinois. He was educated in schools in Ohio and Massachusetts and attended the Cincinnati Art Academy. His early journalism experience was writing publicity releases and book reviews for the *Cincinnati Times-Star* and the *Buffalo Evening News*. In 1935 he began working as a ranch hand in Texas and California and became an expert on breeding quarter horses on his own ranch outside Tucson, Arizona. Much of this love for horses can be found in exceptional novels such as *Wild Horse Shorty* and *Blood of Kings*. He published his first Western short story in *Thrilling Western* and his first Western novel in 1936. He continued from then on to write prolifically, both under his own name and the bylines Drake C. Denver and Clem Colt. During the Second World War, he served with the U.S. Army Field Artillery. In 1949–1952 he worked as horse editor for *Texas Livestock Journal*. He was one of the founding members of the Western Writers of America in 1953 and served twice as its president. His first Golden Spur Award from the Western Writers of America came to him for best Western reviewer and critic in 1954. In 1958–1962 he was frontier fiction reviewer for the *New York Times Book Review*. His second Golden Spur came for his novel *Long Run*. His virtues as an author of Western fiction include a tremendous sense of authenticity, an ability to keep the pace of a story from ever lagging, and a fecund inventiveness for plot twists and situations. Some of his finest novels have had off-trail protagonists such as *The Barber of Tubac*, and both *Not Grass Alone* and *Strawberry Roan* are notable for their outstanding female characters. His books have sold over 50,000,000 copies worldwide and have been translated into the principal European languages. The *Los Angeles Times* once praised him for his "marvelous lingo, salty humor, and real characters." Above all, a Nye Western possesses a vital energy that is both propulsive and persuasive.